SEVENS

WEEK 5:
TORN

Scott Wallens

PUFFIN BOOKS

All quoted materials in this work were created by the author.
Any resemblance to existing works is accidental.

Torn

Puffin Books
Published by the Penguin Group
Penguin Putnam Books for Young Readers,
345 Hudson Street, New York, New York 10014, U.S.A.
Penguin Books Ltd, 80 Strand, London WC2R 0RL, England
Penguin Books Australia Ltd, 250 Camberwell Road, Camberwell, Victoria 3124, Australia
Penguin Books Canada Ltd, 10 Alcorn Avenue, Toronto, Ontario, Canada M4V 3B2
Penguin Books (N.Z.) Ltd, 182-190 Wairau Road, Auckland 10, New Zealand

Penguin Books Ltd, Registered Offices: Harmondsworth, Middlesex, England

Published by Puffin Books,
a division of Penguin Putnam Books for Young Readers, 2002

3 5 7 9 10 8 6 4

Front cover photography copyright © 2001 Karan Kapoor/Stone
Back cover photography copyright (top to bottom) Stewart Cohen/Stone,
David Roth/Stone, David Rinella, Steve Belkowitz/FPG, Karan Kapoor/Stone,
David Lees/FPG, Mary-Arthur Johnson/FPG

 Produced by 17th Street Productions,
an Alloy, Inc. company
151 West 26th Street
New York, NY 10001

17th Street Productions and associated logos
are trademarks and/or registered trademarks of Alloy, Inc.

ISBN 0-14-230102-7

Printed in the United States of America

THIS SERIES IS DEDICATED TO
THE MEMORY OF BLAKE WALLENS,
BELOVED HUSBAND AND FRIEND.

4/16/1970–9/11/2001

CHAPTER ONE

Karyn Aufiero walks into the kitchen Saturday morning, rubbing the sleep from her eyes. She stares out the window above the sink at the small patch of lawn and the nearby cluster of trees. Winter hasn't officially begun, but a layer of frost dusts the ground, and the trees have all lost their leaves.

This is exactly the time of year when Karyn and her father used to collect twigs to make a fire. *Used to.* It's amazing how many of her thoughts about her family contain those two words now that her parents are divorced and her father's moved out. She pictures her dad in the condo he rents along with his girlfriend, Kelly. Kelly, the woman who *used to* live in an apartment above Karyn's dad's dental practice. Kelly, who's barely thirty years old and looks even younger. But that's what Karyn's dad wants—a life full of people and things that are new, untouched. His condo has an ultramodern design with high ceilings, overly large windows, and all brand-new furniture. It's part of why Karyn can't stand visiting him—all that newness, reminding her how easy it was for him to trade in his old life.

Karyn gives her head a quick shake, then turns to gaze around the kitchen. By this time of the morning, her mother is usually seated at the table, cradling her cup of coffee. But today there isn't even any coffee brewing.

Karyn reaches into the cabinet above the sink where the filters are stored. Making coffee isn't her specialty. *I'm sure I can just follow the directions. Why are the stupid filters up so high?* She fumbles around, getting increasingly frustrated. Hastily she pulls her hand down, and three of her mom's vitamin bottles come crashing to the floor.

Oops. Looks like Mom's not sleeping late anymore.

She puts the bottles back in the cabinet, grabs a filter, and starts to make the coffee. One heaping scoop per cup. Not too difficult. She pours in the water, flicks on the pot, then waits until she hears the gurgling sounds.

Karyn sits down at the kitchen table and watches the coffee slowly drip into the pot. She shouldn't have stayed up so late talking on the phone with T. J. But he was all excited because the coach of the Boston College football team told him he was the fastest freshman sprinter he'd ever seen. T. J. sounded like a little boy who had just won season tickets to Disneyland. Karyn smiles. That's exactly what she loves about her boyfriend. When he's happy, he oozes happiness. It's contagious.

She looks over at the time on the microwave. Ten after nine. *There's no way Mom's still asleep. Not after all that noise.*

She gets up and leaves the coffee, walking up the stairs to her mother's bedroom.

"Mom?" Karyn says, giving the door a light tap.

Nothing.

"Mom," she repeats, gently pushing open the door. "Are you a—"

Karyn stops, stunned by what she sees. Or actually, what she doesn't see, which is her mom in the perfectly made bed. A ray of sunlight falls on a plain white pillow, directly on the spot where Ms. Aufiero's head should be. But isn't. And obviously hasn't been all night.

Karyn's muscles tense, but she can't take her eyes off the pillow. Most daughters would be worried if they saw an empty bed. Daughters with normal mothers, not a mother who started playing musical beds with a ridiculous number of men ever since her divorce was final. A lump forms in Karyn's throat, and she's overwhelmed by a rush of disgust and anger.

Who is it this time? That banker guy Neil? Maybe the pseudo-intellectual William? Or *Wilhelm,* as he had corrected her mother when she introduced him.

Suddenly Karyn wants to get as far away from her mother's bedroom as possible. She turns around and walks back down to the kitchen. With a shaky hand she pours herself a cup of coffee, then sits down at the table. Why does it still get to her so much? She wishes she could just ignore it, not care. But every time her mom comes home on the arm of some new guy,

3

Karyn feels like *she's* the one who should be mortified. Maybe because she knows someone should be, and that someone doesn't seem to be her mom, the most screwed-up high school guidance counselor in the history of time. God, what would the kids at school think if they knew that this woman sitting there giving them advice was such a mess herself?

Karyn winces. A few times she's had to make up an excuse to uninvite Amy or Gemma from coming over, just to avoid them seeing her mom show up late at night with some freaky guy.

Karyn kicks her feet up onto a chair. When her parents first split up, she felt terrible for her mom. She couldn't even begin to understand what it would feel like to watch your twenty-year marriage come to an end and then see your husband move in with some beautiful younger woman. But then her mom started dating again after, like, two seconds. And as hard as she tried, Karyn couldn't sympathize. Seeing her mom act as trashy as some of the girls in her school? It just wasn't something she could deal with.

Karyn plans what she'll say when her mom gets home. *I called the cops and filed a missing persons report. You're gonna be in next week's police blotter.* Or, *You've had a million phone calls. I told everyone you didn't come home last night.*

The clock on the microwave says nine-twenty. Karyn sits up with a start.

I'm supposed to meet Reed for brunch at ten to work on college applications. I can't believe I almost forgot.

Karyn jumps up and pours her coffee down the drain, her mood doing a complete one-eighty. A day hanging out with her best friend is exactly what she needs right now. He's the only person who really knows what Karyn's mom has been like this past year since the divorce. She's way too embarrassed to tell the rest of her friends or even T. J. What if her boyfriend wondered if being a pathetic slut ran in the genes? He might not admit it, but somewhere inside he'd feel disgusted with her for what her mom does. How could he not? Besides, what's cool about T. J. is that he's sort of programmed for the positive stuff, not to sit around talking about problems. He likes to hear about Falls High football games or plans for a school dance, and he was even more psyched than she was when she made it onto the varsity cheerleading squad her junior year.

But she and T. J.'s little brother, Reed, have been friends forever, and he knows everything about her. He knew her back when her favorite thing to do was sit in mud puddles (something he didn't forget to bring up—in private—when she ended up on the homecoming court as a junior last year). So maybe that's why it doesn't bug her for him to know all her deep, dark secrets. And he's just good at figuring out what to say, too. It's what makes him such a great friend.

Karyn slides Madonna's *Greatest Hits* into her stereo and dances around in front of her closet, searching for something to wear. *Just a ray of light . . .*

She pulls on a pair of dark blue boot-cut jeans with a

gray V-neck sweater, then applies a thin layer of lip gloss. Once she's ready, Karyn grabs a large shopping bag full of college catalogs and applications from under her bed. On top of the pile is the one for Boston College. T. J.'s school. Of course it's on her list.

Karyn traces her fingers over the words *Boston College*. She hasn't told anybody that she's thinking of applying there, not even T. J. Karyn takes the catalog out of the bag and puts it under the bed.

If I show this to Reed, he'll tell T. J. Not a good idea.

Once T. J. hears she's applying there, he'll go crazy and start making plans, like where they'll meet up for lunches next fall. She loves how much he wants to be with her all the time, and she feels the same way. It's why she's seriously considering going there. But she can't help thinking what a major step that would be. If she moves there for school, they'll practically end up living together. And right now they haven't . . .well, they haven't even had sex yet. In fact, Karyn hasn't had sex, period. Which seems pretty ironic considering how much time she spends *thinking* about having sex. Wondering whether she should, how long T. J. will be willing to wait for her . . .

Karyn stands up, holding the bag full of applications. She really needs to calm down. She's stressing for nothing— T. J.'s not rushing her. He would never pressure her.

Karyn pushes all thoughts of Boston and living together and sex from her mind. She takes one last look in the mirror, narrowing her eyes as she adjusts her shirt.

Why are you so worried about what you're wearing? It's just Reed.

She glances at the clock on her bedside table as she rushes out of the room. So she's going to be ten minutes late. Reed won't get worked up. He never does. He's always just as psyched to see her as she is to see him.

• • •

"You're gonna go into a food coma if you don't slow down," Karyn jokes as she watches Reed stuff half a pancake into his mouth.

Reed looks up and smiles. He wipes a drop of syrup from his chin.

"Real classy," she says, digging into a pile of home fries.

Reed chokes on a laugh once he manages to swallow some of the pancake, then takes a swig of orange juice to help wash it down. Yeah, he's pretty hungry. But the main reason he's scarfing down his breakfast is to give himself something to take his mind off Karyn and how incredible she looks right now. Which is impossible, anyway, considering she's sitting right across from him at the Falls Diner, facing him with her toothpaste commercial smile and gorgeous eyes.

Man, you have got to stop thinking like this about Karyn. She's your best friend. She's your brother's girlfriend.

It's become like a mantra for him—*your brother's girl-friend, your brother's girlfriend.* He zings the words at himself all the time, hoping they'll finally destroy these feelings he can't stop having for the one girl in the universe who is absolutely off-limits. But so far, it's not doing much. It doesn't help that every time he's around her, she manages to find some new way to prove how right she is for him.

Reed straightens his baseball cap and tries to focus his attention elsewhere. But no matter what he does, there's a pit the size of the Grand Canyon in his gut. And his mind keeps conjuring these images of T. J., causing the guilt to get worse by the minute. Like the mountain-biking trip they took to Yosemite last spring. It was just the two of them, hard-core biking for three days. Reed flipped head-first over his handlebars on the last day. Nothing was broken, but he'd gotten the wind knocked out of him and was pretty dizzy. T. J. cleaned and bandaged his cuts. Made sure they took an easier route back to the lodge. Watching out for Reed is just part of T. J.'s nature. Whereas being a back-stabbing evil brother is obviously part of Reed's.

"Hey, space cadet," Karyn says, kicking Reed's shin under the table. "Don't tell me you really are going into a food coma."

Reed snaps himself out of his daze and turns his attention to Karyn. Her blue eyes stare back at him.

"Huh? I could polish off another order of pancakes easy."

Karyn shakes her head and places a forkful of her spinach-and feta-omelette in her mouth.

God, she even looks cute when she eats.

He looks down at his watch, just to have somewhere else to rest his gaze.

"What, am I taking too long?" Karyn asks. "Sorry, I decided not to try and beat your record of a full breakfast consumed in under a minute."

Reed looks up and grins. "No, it's just we have work to do. Remember?"

Karyn sighs. "Okay, you caught me. I'm stalling. Are we really going to work *all* afternoon?" she asks, giving him a pleading look.

"What else did you think we were gonna do?"

Karyn playfully tilts her head to the side. "Ohhh, I don't know. How about a movie at the Triplex?"

Reed narrows his eyes at her in a fake glare. This is so Karyn. The same Karyn who talked him into blowing off studying for a math midterm and kept him at the diner until eleven the night before an AP history test.

"No way," he says. "We're going to the library after this. We're working."

Karyn giggles. "Whatever."

Reed waits, knowing she never gives in so easily.

"I just know how much you like movies," she adds.

"I'll make a deal with you," Reed suggests.

"What's that?"

"Applications today. Movie tonight."

Karyn crosses her arms and pretends to think about it. "Okay, you've got a deal. But promise we can take a coffee break from studying later, maybe get cappuccino at Geoffrey's?"

"Promise."

Reed signals their waitress, Norma, for the check. He pulls a Michigan catalog from his backpack—one of the schools he's seriously considering. Karyn takes the catalog and immediately flips to a picture of the football field.

"This is gonna be you. You'll be starting as a freshman, I'm positive," she says with total confidence.

Reed's insides turn to mush. Karyn always manages to say exactly what he needs to hear. Everyone else expects him to go to an Ivy League. "With your grades, why would you even think about anything else?" everyone says. But Karyn knows how badly he wants to go to a football school. She gets how much he loves the sport.

Norma stops by their table and drops the check directly in front of Reed. "Here you go," she says. "I like to make the boyfriends pay," she adds, giving Karyn a smile.

"Ha!" Karyn exclaims as Norma walks away. "Did you hear that, boyfriend? I guess brunch is on you."

A gigantic lump fills Reed's throat. He keeps his eyes glued to the Michigan football field. If he looks hard enough, maybe Norma's comment will disappear.

"Or not?" Karyn waves a hand in front of Reed's face.

He looks up. Beads of sweat pop up on his palms. "Uh, yeah. I got this one. No big deal."

"Thanks," Karyn says, standing up. "I'll get snacks for

the movie. I'm just going to stop in the bathroom. Don't worry, I'll be fast."

Reed's eyes start to follow her, but he pulls his gaze away. What's it going to take for him to get over this?

• • •

On a regular Saturday morning, Jane Scott has a million things to do besides sleep. But not this Saturday morning. It's nearly ten-thirty, and she's in desperate need of toothpaste, but the last thing she wants to do is get up.

She opens her eyes and stares at the dull gray sky outside her window, playing back last night's drama in her mind. Her parents know she's a fake. All that time spent studying for Academic Decathlon, working on papers, writing articles for the Web site, practicing her sax—it all turned to nothing in an instant. Now they know the truth—she's a failure. And a liar.

Jane slides further into the safety of her bed, trying to distance herself from the memory of last night. She vaguely recalls the total mental exhaustion that overtook her after the confrontation was over. Finally she had told her parents the truth about the SATs. Pulled the thin piece of paper out from under her mattress and showed them her score. A whopping 200. And they'd reacted . . . well, basically the way she'd expected. Until the part where she told them to leave her room, and they actually did.

She'd been so exhausted afterward, she'd crashed right away. Then, sometime later, she'd woken up to the sound of

11

shouts. "Academic Decathlon . . . SAT scores . . . Harvard . . . Boston Conservatory . . . audition tape . . ." Each syllable of her parents' angry voices stung. "If you hadn't been so adamant about Harvard and MIT . . . Letting her play the saxophone all day when she should have been doing something worthwhile. . . . Worthwhile! If you paid any attention, you'd see how gifted she is with music. . . ."

Jane had gotten up to go to the bathroom, feeling ill. Why wouldn't they let up? Ever since her parents' divorce when she was twelve, they'd barely been able to function in the same room. Now, it seemed, they couldn't get away, couldn't stop railing into each other.

Jane stayed in the bathroom for a long time. The nausea came and went, but somehow she couldn't manage the energy to get up even when she felt okay. Eventually she had heard the front door open and close. Her father had finally left. Then she'd gotten up and returned to her room. To her bed, which is where she's been ever since, wishing she could stay here forever.

Jane lies still, watching the clouds move past her window. She doesn't know how much time has passed before she hears a light tapping on her door.

"Jane, are you awake?"

Suddenly her exhaustion is replaced with panic as the reality of what's coming hits her. Now that her father is gone, her mother will start in on her. She'll want answers, and Jane isn't sure she has them.

"I'm up, Mom," she calls out. She sits up and swings her legs over the side of the bed.

The door opens a crack. "I just wanted to see how you were doing."

"I'm okay," Jane answers, standing and smoothing down her hair.

Jane's mom steps into the bedroom. She looks as well put together as ever in tan pressed slacks and a brown sweater. There's little indication of what she went through last night, except for the puffiness around her eyes that even her makeup can't quite conceal. She smiles. "Sweetie, I hope—I hope we didn't keep you up at all last night."

Jane stares at her, wondering what to say, what's next.

Ms. Scott lets out a small sigh, then walks over and sits down on the bed. She glances at Jane and pats the comforter next to her. Jane hesitantly sits, somehow not wanting this conversation to take place in the one spot where she's felt safe in the past twenty-four hours.

"I'm sorry that your father and I—that things didn't go very well last night," Jane's mom begins. "You have to understand, I was just so shocked. Your scores, it was the last thing either of us expected to hear, of course. And I really wish I could understand what happened. . . ." She trails off, looking at Jane with *the* question in her eyes. She wants to know what happened to her real daughter. The one who's brilliant and talented and perfect and never lets her down. She wants Jane

13

to explain where that daughter went and when this one, the failure with no future, moved in.

Jane tears her gaze away and looks down at the floor, pressing her lips together. She can't talk about it, about that day in the gym when she ruined her whole life. Not yet. It was hard enough just showing her parents the scores.

"Well, okay, honey," Ms. Scott says awkwardly after a moment of silence. "I guess you're not ready to—I mean, you must be very tired. We can talk more later. Right now, you just need to relax. I've made a nice breakfast, so why don't you come down and have something to eat? I'm sure getting food in your stomach will help you feel better."

Jane raises her eyes to meet her mother's, feeling a flicker of something she hasn't experienced in as long as she can remember—hope. Is her mom going to ease up on her now? Did Jane actually get through to her last night?

Ms. Scott stands up. "There's sausage and eggs, so go ahead and wash up so you can come downstairs before it gets cold."

Jane nods slowly, in total disbelief.

Her mother is almost out the door when she turns around, leaning against the door frame. "Jane, I just need to tell you something," she says.

Jane cringes. Here it comes.

"I want you to hear that I know this isn't your fault."

Jane's eyes widen. She's dreaming, right? This is just too unbelievable to be real.

14

"It's just—I've tried to make your father understand how much pressure he puts on you," her mom continues. "He never understands how important your music is to you, that you need more time for it. All that talk about Harvard, Yale—I know what he's done to you, and I promise I won't let it keep happening."

Right, of course. That small twinge of hope is gone before Jane has a chance to really remember what the emotion feels like. The reason her mom isn't mad at her for screwing up isn't that she actually understands or heard a word Jane said last night. It's that she blames Jane's dad, just like she blames him for everything. She would blame him for world hunger if she could find a way.

"I don't want you to worry about this, Jane. We'll figure something out, we'll make sure you can still get into one of the conservatories you've dreamed about. After breakfast we'll talk about how you can retake the SATs. And then we'll think about which of your activities you can drop, starting with the Web site, and then maybe the Academic Decathlon team, and . . ."

Jane stops listening as her mother goes on, listing everything that's important to her dad. She'd been scared of what would happen when she told her parents the truth. Terrified that everything would change. But now she realizes that nothing is going to change. And that's much, much worse.

• • •

"This is a must have," Gemma Masters declares, pulling a long denim coat off the clothing rack in the Winetka Falls Mall's Contempo Casuals store Saturday afternoon.

"A little country western, don't you think?" Karyn comments, noting the rhinestone studs on the sleeves.

Gemma puts on the coat. "I need to add some spice to my wardrobe."

Karyn rolls her eyes at Amy Santisi, who smiles back. They both know how Gemma gets. Out of boredom, she'll switch personas practically overnight. Lately she's been doing the classic Audrey Hepburn look. It's now obvious she's making the move toward Britney Spears.

Karyn can usually spend hours browsing the racks with her friends. It's a chance to combine two of her favorite activities—gossiping and shopping. But this afternoon, she's distracted. She left Reed a little over an hour ago after barely completing more than a few general information sections on her applications. She'd just gotten too restless, sitting there in the library in total silence with Reed. He wouldn't even lift his head from those stupid applications for five seconds. And when she managed to smuggle two cappuccinos past the librarian, all he said was, "You're gonna get us kicked out of here."

After that, Karyn told him she was going to take a bathroom break. Instead she went and called Amy on her cell phone. Amy said she and Gemma were going to the mall, and Karyn told her she'd meet them there. When she told Reed, he gave her a quick look. "Okay," he'd said.

Okay? Not a single protest?

Karyn picks up a cashmere scarf from the accessory table and runs her fingers along it, wondering what put him in such a bad mood. Even at the diner, he was sort of spacey. That was actually why she never brought up the thing with her mom—he didn't seem to be in the right place to listen to anything intense. Maybe he was just stressing about the college stuff more than he admitted, although that was pretty silly, considering he has amazing grades along with being a star quarterback.

"Rhinestones belong in Texas, Gemma," Amy warns.

"Well, it's about time someone brought them to Winetka Falls."

Amy gives her an exasperated sigh. "Let's go somewhere else."

"Fine," Gemma says, putting the coat back.

Outside the store, the three walk leisurely through the brightly lit mall. The place is mobbed with weekend shoppers. Children with their moms, cute couples holding hands, and clusters of teenagers.

"This is where we need to go," Gemma says, tugging Karyn and Amy toward Victoria's Secret. The second they walk in, the strong flowery scent fills Karyn's nose.

"Over here," Gemma says, leading them to a rack of lacy camisoles with matching underwear. "Carlos got me this," she announces proudly.

"You mean he picked this out alone?" Amy asks.

17

Gemma nods.

Karyn fingers the black lace sewn onto the pale pink silk. Tiny sequins are embroidered along the edges. It's more tacky than pretty. "Do you like it?" she asks.

"Oh, come on." Gemma lowers her voice and leans in close to Amy and Karyn. "A guy gets what *he* likes. It's all part of the fantasy."

The fantasy. Does T. J. have one? If he does, Karyn has no idea what it is. And what about her own? Lacy lingerie doesn't usually factor in. She figures losing her virginity will have to come before the sexy underwear.

And that's something she's definitely fantasized about. For some reason she always pictures an old farmhouse in the middle of a snowy field, with a wood-burning fireplace inside and a plush warm comforter they're lying under. . . .

Karyn blushes and turns away from her friends. It's pretty sappy, she knows, but that's what she wants her first time to be like. Completely romantic and safe. In a way, shouldn't that be what sex *always* feels like? Karyn can't help thinking of her mom, who has had more sexual partners in the past few months than Karyn wants to remember, and not one of them has seemed romantic. Is that what happens with sex after the first time? Or even *for* the first time? Gemma's descriptions of her and Carlos don't sound very romantic.

"Maybe we should buy you one of these," Gemma says, interrupting her thoughts. "T. J. seems like a total lingerie guy."

"Forget it," Karyn replies. She is so not in the mood for another when-will-you-sleep-with-T. J. conversation.

Gemma picks up a purple bra decorated with flowers. "What I want to know is when you're going to put those condoms you bought to use."

Karyn groans.

"Don't tell me," Gemma teases. "You brought them back to the drugstore."

"Oh, leave the poor girl alone," Amy says.

"I'm just looking out for your interests," Gemma protests. "College guys don't hold out forever."

"Are you done discussing my sex life?" Karyn snaps.

"Don't let her get to you," Amy says. "T. J. is totally devoted. You're lucky."

Karyn knows she's lucky. T. J. *is* devoted. He would never come and go like her mom's dates. Which is why she has to stop stressing so much about sex. Her mother is the one who's made the mistakes, not Karyn.

CHAPTER TWO

"Ready, sweetheart?" Peter Davis's mother says, opening the car door. Beside her is his wheelchair. It's Saturday afternoon and they're in Meena Miller's driveway.

"Ready," he answers. He's so anxious to find out how Meena is, he doesn't even mind as his mother helps maneuver him into the wheelchair. Every second that's gone by since he was here on Thursday has passed at an agonizingly slow rate. Meena all but admitted that she'd been sexually abused by Peter's own neighbor, Steven Clayton. He can't stand thinking about it, wondering what really happened to her and if she's okay—especially with Clayton living in her house.

"I'll wait if you want," his mother says with a frown.

Peter looks at the closed front door. "No, Meena will drive me home," he says, deciding to take a risk. He'd called her about a half hour ago, telling her he was on his way over. Not asking. Telling. Yesterday at school, Meena had gone out of her way to avoid him. But he couldn't let this go, not after the way she'd broken down on Thursday, so obviously terrified of Clayton.

His mother hesitates. Peter can tell she's confused by this second emergency drive over to Meena's in one week. "We're just hanging out," he says lamely.

"Okay, honey. We'll see you at home." She walks around to the driver's side and gets in the car.

Peter wheels himself toward the Millers' front door. What's he going to say to her? How can he get her to tell him what's really going on? Just as he's about to ring the bell, the front door opens. He looks up and sees Meena staring down at him, her expression blank.

"Hey, Peter," she says, lifting the corners of her mouth in a weak attempt at a smile.

"Hey," he says cautiously. "I hope you don't mind that I came over."

"No," she says, walking behind his chair and helping him through the entrance. "I'm not doing anything."

"Are you . . . are you okay?" he asks. *Stupid question. Of course she's not okay. She hasn't been in weeks.*

Meena walks around to face him. "Yeah, I'm okay."

Peter hears voices from the living room. He peers around Meena and sees Steven and Lydia Clayton. They're arguing about the best way to dismantle a crib. Steven looks up and gives Peter a strange look. At least, it seems like a strange look to Peter, since how could the guy not be wary of him after that weird scene on Thursday night?

21

"Come on," Meena mutters. She wheels Peter down the hall into the kitchen. They sit there silently for a moment, and Peter feels ready to scream.

"I know the other day was—well, I got upset," Meena finally says. She starts twisting her silver thumb ring around her finger. "I just . . . I wasn't getting along with Steven." She glances over her shoulder. "But now things are better."

"Better?" Peter asks skeptically.

"Yeah, the Claytons are moving out." At this point her voice has dropped to a whisper.

"Oh?" Peter says.

Meena tries for another smile, but it's even worse than the first one. Her brown eyes are still full of the same fear he saw on Thursday, and her hands are trembling. "Their house isn't going to be repaired for a while," she explains. "So they're going to rent one. Tonight is their last night here." On the last sentence, he hears genuine relief.

Peter thinks of Steven's clean-cut appearance, how right now he's just a guy dismantling his kid's crib. *I'd like to wheel right in there and dismantle the jerk's face.* Peter's hands clench into fists, then relax in his lap as he realizes that he's being an idiot. The only reason he wants to beat the guy up is that it's something he could *do* for Meena since he feels so helpless. But he knows what she really needs is for him to listen, to let her tell him what happened and get her help.

"Peter," Meena says, grabbing his arm as if she knows what he's thinking. "Everything is fine, I swear."

Her gaze is urgent, pleading, but what Peter sees is that her eyes are bloodshot, with deep circles beneath them. A sickly yellow tinge clouds her complexion.

This girl is not fine. She's a mess.

Meena starts playing with the ring again. "They're leaving. That's what's important."

"Meena," he says quietly. "I know something happened. You can tell me, you can—"

"They're leaving," she hisses, cutting him off. "Don't you get it? It's over now. Please, just—please stop."

But he can't, even though the sound of her voice cracking in pain rips into him. This is too major. "It's not going to disappear, even if he moves out," Peter continues gently. "I don't know what he did, Meena, but whatever it is, you can't let him get away with it. You've got to tell someone."

Meena's eyes glisten with tears. Peter can almost feel her terror inside him. It's overwhelming. But he knows he's right—he knows Meena won't get better just because Steven Clayton leaves her house. He's no expert on this stuff, and he still doesn't know exactly what Clayton did to her, but he's heard his dad talk about sexual abuse cases enough to know how long it takes the victims to get better, especially if they don't deal with what happened to them.

Wait. That's who needs to help Meena here. The cops.

"What about the police?" he asks, leaning forward.

Meena pales. Shakes her head. "No way," she says.

23

She stares at him with her scared eyes, and he flashes back to another moment like this one, another time when they talked about calling the police, and she was just as afraid. He wonders if she's remembering, too.

Meena clears her throat. "Peter, please. The Claytons are moving. And my brothers are even coming home this week, for Thanksgiving break. I'll be okay."

But you're not okay. Not even close.

"Just promise you won't tell anyone?"

Reluctantly he nods.

• • •

Karyn turns up the volume on her radio, then returns to the mess in her closet and digs around for something to wear. She's glad she and Reed have plans to go to the movies tonight. Hopefully he'll be feeling better about the college stuff after putting in a lot of hours on his applications, and they can relax and have fun.

Karyn pulls on a pair of black suede jeans and holds up the new sweater Gemma and Amy convinced her to buy at the mall. It's a red cowl neck, loose at the throat and extra fitted around the body.

"Great color."

Karyn turns around. Ms. Aufiero is standing in the doorway, wearing a black skirt that's an inch or two shy of decent for her age and knee-high boots. On top she's wearing nothing but a camisole right now. It's pink with black trim. The exact same camisole that Carlos bought for

Gemma. The thought of her mother wearing the same lingerie as her friend makes her ill.

"Which blouse? The black or the purple?" Ms. Aufiero holds up the two choices and waits for Karyn's response.

Karyn stiffens. They haven't spoken all day. Not since Karyn got back from the mall and found her mother camped out on the couch in her bathrobe. The tired circles under her eyes were proof of the kind of night she'd had. Karyn avoided any confrontation by saying a quick hello and then hurrying up to her bedroom. She'd wanted her mom to know she was pissed at her for not coming home, but apparently the message hadn't come through.

"Well?" her mother prompts.

"I don't like either," Karyn says, turning back to her closet. Bad enough that her mom didn't come home after last night's date. Tonight she's got another one. And she wants Karyn to act as fashion consultant?

"No?" her mom says, the hurt in her voice making Karyn's shoulders tense. It's so sick—she says these things, knowing they'll get to her mom and *wanting* that to happen. But she still feels bad when it works.

It's just, ever since the divorce, her mom has been treating Karyn like they're friends, not mother and daughter. Karyn already has plenty of friends—ones her own age who don't sleep in strange men's beds on a regular basis.

Karyn turns to her mom, hardening her expression.

25

"You should stick with jeans, Mom. It's what most women your age wear on a Saturday night."

There's a quick, momentary flinch in response, but then Ms. Aufiero crosses her arms in front of the thin camisole. "I don't see why anyone should have to dress a certain way because of their age," she argues.

Karyn shakes her head. "Yeah, I guess you wouldn't," she says. "Since you also don't see what's wrong with sleeping in different beds every night."

Ms. Aufiero's mouth falls slightly open, and she stares back at Karyn in shock. Then her eyes flare in anger. "You cannot speak to me like that," she says. "I am still your mother, you know."

Karyn lets out a harsh laugh. "Right," she says. The phone on her nightstand rings. Karyn reaches for the receiver, hoping it's Reed. "Hello?" she says.

"Hi, sweetheart, it's Dad."

"Hi, Dad," Karyn says a little too loudly, watching the way her mom seems to sag when she hears the words. "What's up?"

Ms. Aufiero pauses awkwardly for a moment in the doorway, then turns and retreats down the hall, leaving Karyn feeling a familiar mixture of triumph and guilt.

"I wanted to let you know that Kelly is going to join us for our Thanksgiving celebration on Tuesday," her dad says. "She's really excited, honey."

"Tuesday?" Karyn echoes.

"Yes—I asked you last week and you said Tuesday was

26

fine. Remember, sweetie? This way you can spend the actual day with your mom."

Wonderful. Tuesday with her dad and his girl toy Kelly, and Thursday with her wanna-be girl toy mom.

"Karyn, are you there?"

"Yeah, Dad, I'm here," she replies softly.

"Is everything okay?"

"Yeah, fine." Karyn wishes she could turn back the clock. She remembers when Thanksgiving used to be fun. *Used to, again.*

They'd spend the morning cooking and the afternoon eating. Afterward they'd take an early evening walk. Her father would carry Karyn on his back and wrap an arm around her mother. She remembers thinking that her life would look identical when she got married. She's not sure exactly when things went bad. He started missing dinners and going away to dental conventions all the time. And the fights . . . they had kept Karyn awake for hours. Her mom would always end up in tears, and it got to the point where Karyn wondered why her mother even wanted to be married anymore when she was always so unhappy. Except that somehow even that constant fighting and crying had to be better than being alone. But eventually it hadn't been up to her, anyway, because Mr. Aufiero had made the decision to leave her.

Karyn clears her throat. She wants to tell him no, it's not okay for Kelly to join them. It's not okay for him to expect her to accept his brand-new life with a smile.

"Sure, Dad. It's fine if Kelly joins us," she says, biting her lip.

"Good, sweetie. She's a great cook, so plan to come with an empty stomach."

"Great," she says.

"I'll be in the neighborhood, so why don't I just pick you up at seven?"

The call-waiting beep sounds. "Dad, someone's on the other line. I've gotta go."

"Seven, then," her dad says quickly.

"Sure, see you then. Bye." She presses the flash button. "Hello?"

"Hey, Karyn."

His voice is like an instant muscle relaxant, and she shuts her eyes, relieved. "Hey, Reed," she says.

"You guys do a lot of damage at the mall?" he asks.

Karyn smiles. "I wasn't too bad. Gemma, of course, is a different story. So what's up for tonight?"

"Well, that's what I wanted to talk to you about."

Karyn frowns.

"The thing is, I'm actually really beat. And I think I'm coming down with a cold. I can't risk getting sick and missing the next game. So I think I'd better stay home."

Karyn wraps the phone cord around her fingers.

"Are you mad?" he asks.

"No, of course not," she says, trying to hide her disappointment. "You shouldn't go out if you don't feel well."

"I'm sorry for screwing up your plans. Maybe you can hang out with Amy or Gemma."

"No, I'll probably stay home, too," she says. She knows he wouldn't lie to her, but she can't help wondering . . . is he really sick, or does he just not want to hang out? Why is he being so different around her lately?

"Sorry," he says.

"Don't worry about it. Just feel better. I'll talk to you later."

"Thanks, Karyn. Bye."

Karyn hangs up, then lies down on her bed and stares at the grooves in the ceiling. Her room suddenly seems gigantic. Now what's she going to do tonight? Lie here all by herself for hours? Her friends all have plans already. *Why does T. J. have to be so far away?*

Frustrated, Karyn rolls over and picks up her phone again. She dials T. J.'s number. The phone rings . . . one . . . two . . . three . . .

"Hello?"

She can barely hear him with all the noise in the background. There's lots of voices—male *and* female voices.

"Hey, Teej, it's me," she says. "What's going on over there?"

"Sorry, everyone's just getting ready to head over to a party," he explains. "It gets crazy here on Saturdays."

"Oh." Crazy, like lots-of-girls-all-over-her-boyfriend crazy? Karyn sighs, willing herself to stop being paranoid. "I just called because I—well, I miss you," she says.

29

"Oh, babe, I miss you, too," he says. "Hey, watch it, that's an expensive stereo," he yells at someone on his end.

"I wish I could be there with you," she adds.

"Yeah, me too. What are you up to tonight?"

Karyn flips over her pillow, playing with the edge. "Nothing, really."

"You should get out—do something with Amy or one of your other friends. Or what about my loser brother? Maybe you can get him out of the house. That guy spends way too much time studying."

Karyn suddenly feels an intense wave of sadness. Probably just that she misses T. J. so much.

"Well, you should probably go, right?" she says, her grip on the phone tightening.

No, Karyn—I'm not going to the party if you're stuck at home. I'll stay here and talk to you so you don't have to be alone.

"Yeah, I've gotta bolt. I'm really sorry—you know I'd rather be with you than at some party."

"Uh-huh," she says, staring up at the ceiling.

"Listen, I'll call you tomorrow, I promise."

"Okay. Bye, Teej."

"Hey, Karyn?"

"Yeah?"

"I love you," he says, and she can hear the smile in his voice.

She starts to say it back, but stops when she hears the dial tone in her ear.

• • •

Reed takes a bite of his egg roll, savoring the way the sweet and salty flavors combine in his mouth. The crispy, flaky egg rolls are his favorite thing here at The Cottage, a cheap Chinese restaurant frequented by anyone who's lived in Winetka Falls long enough to know that the food is much more appetizing than the decor.

Across from Reed, Jeremy Mandile masterfully uses his chopsticks to eat a plate of fried rice. Neither of them speaks—they're too engrossed in their food. Besides, they're together practically twenty-four seven. Jeremy's parents still haven't caved and asked him to move back home or told him they're okay with the fact that he's gay. At least they let him hang out with his sister, Emily, sometimes. Reed knows Jeremy would really lose it if he didn't get to see his little sister. Sort of the way Reed would feel if he couldn't talk to Karyn.

Not that anyone would be able to guess that from the way he'd stood her up to come to dinner with someone he spends plenty of time with already.

He'd meant it this morning when he said they should see a movie tonight. But then he couldn't get that comment Norma made out of his head. It's not like whatever the Falls Diner waitstaff thinks about the two of them really matters, but what's scary is that anyone could mistake them for a couple so easily. Well, what's scary is how easy it would be for *him* to make that mistake. So he needed some breathing room. A movie just felt too much like a date.

"So did you finish your applications?" Jeremy asks, wiping a spot of grease off his chin.

"Pretty much. I've still gotta do Michigan."

"Does your mom know you're not going strictly Ivy League?" Jeremy asks.

"Not yet." Reed laces his fingers and cracks his knuckles. "But if I wanna play real football, I've gotta go to a real football school. How else am I gonna get the exposure?"

"I can just see it," Jeremy says. "Reed Frasier, the next Heisman Trophy winner. I knew him when . . ."

"I wish." Reed snorts. "Odds of me getting into a major athletic school are pretty slim. I didn't even start until this year." He reaches across the table for the rice.

"Not because you weren't good enough," Jeremy says. "Come on, man, you gave up the chance. Not many guys would do that. Even for their brother. Once the scouts see what you can do, you'll be on the top of their lists."

Reed shrugs. Maybe he shouldn't have told Jeremy and Karyn about the championship game last year. The game that won T. J. Athlete of the Year, which never would have happened if Reed had agreed to let Coach start him instead of faking sick and staying home.

Reed fills his plate with more food, then pours heaps of hot mustard on top.

"Whoa, you trying to set yourself on fire?" Jeremy laughs.

Reed grunts as he takes a huge mouthful of food. After

a few bites, his mouth starts to burn. He forces himself to chew and swallow. He just wants to eat. Not talk about college, football—any of it. Lately it's like everywhere he turns, he keeps bumping into T. J.'s life. First football, now Karyn. Finding another direction to move in is getting harder all the time.

The door swings open and Reed whips his head around. What if Karyn made last minute plans with her friends to come to The Cottage? But it's not Karyn. Just Danny Chaiken and Cori Lerner.

"Hey, Danny, Cori. What's up?" Jeremy says.

"Hey, guys," Danny replies.

"I guess we were all thinking the same thing tonight," Cori says, glancing at the plate of egg rolls. "I'm starving."

"Ooh, sorry. Mr. Ling over there said we took the last order," Jeremy teases.

"Then I guess we'll have to grab some of yours," Danny replies with a grin.

"Feel free," Reed adds. "Just be prepared to pay a small fee." He looks back and forth between Cori and Danny, noticing they're holding hands. Must be a new couple. Not one he would have predicted, but seeing them together makes sense. She's sort of funky and free spirited. And Danny's definitely a free spirit.

Danny points to a table that's just being cleared. "There's an empty booth. We'd better grab it."

Cori waves good-bye as Danny takes her elbow, guiding her across the restaurant.

"See ya," Reed and Jeremy call out.

"Danny and Cori," Jeremy says. "Who knew?"

"Yeah," Reed agrees, watching them sit down. They both have that ready-to-burst-from-happiness look of a new couple in love.

Is that how T. J. and Karyn look when they're out together? Reed shakes his head. He can't do this to himself anymore. But he also can't give up his friendship with Karyn. Not being with her tonight sure hasn't stopped him from thinking about her, so obviously ditching her isn't the best solution. No, he's just got to make himself get over her—for good.

• • •

Karyn runs through the woods. Overhead, the black sky is partially lit by the moon. She can barely see where she's going. Tree branches slap her face. Snow crunches beneath her feet, but despite the winter chill, she's sweating. Something—someone—is chasing her. She looks around frantically, hoping to see the window of her house, maybe Reed's face, something familiar. Something safe.

She pumps her legs faster. Speed is her only chance. Maybe if she turns around, faces whatever's behind her . . .

No. Can't turn around.

Something tells her she knows exactly who or what is following her. And once she sees it for sure, then she'll know nothing in her life will ever be safe. It never was.

A rock catches her foot and her body hurtles through the air.

Falling . . . falling . . . she braces herself for the moment of impact. But the falling never ends. She's alone in the dark, like being trapped inside a black hole. At some point Karyn realizes that she's surrounded by stillness. She's no longer falling, and the thing chasing her has disappeared. She fumbles around for the cold, wet earth. It's gone. Slowly Karyn opens one eye, then the other. She's lying on a cement floor. It's somebody's basement. The sour stench of mold fills her nostrils and she presses an arm to her face to block the smell. But it's no use. The odor slides down her throat and she begins to choke. Soon her entire body is racked with coughs.

Air, she needs fresh air. She gets on her hands and knees. A staircase leads up to a door. A single lightbulb sways overhead. The place is familiar. When was she last here? A terrible dread fills her body. Worse than when she was in the woods. In the woods she could run. In this place she's trapped.

Footsteps. Lots of them. They're coming from above. Karyn looks to the door just as it swings open. Three tall figures framed by a light begin to descend. Karyn can't turn or run. She can't . . . wait! She knows those figures. They're people she trusts. Her father is in front, followed by T. J. and Reed.

Her father is the first to step into the circle of light. When he's close enough, he extends a hand and Karyn grabs it. Instantly she knows something is wrong. T. J. extends his hand and she takes his, too. Suddenly the basement grows colder.

Karyn tries to wrench herself free, but her father and T. J. are too strong. Where's Reed? Reed can help her.

He steps into the light. Karyn relaxes at the familiar sight of his baseball cap. She looks at him with pleading eyes.

Do something.

Reed just stands there, staring at her. His gaze is cold. It tells her that she's done something terrible. Unforgivable.

What did I do?

Nobody speaks. Terrified, Karyn twists and turns, trying to pull herself free. But T. J. and her father hold on tight.

Why are you doing this? Please let me go.

Karyn begins to cry. She wants to wrap herself into a tight ball and hide in a corner. Finally she manages to free herself. She races for the stairs but stumbles on something. Someone. She looks behind her and sees Peter Davis. He's ten. He's crying, too.

Karyn tries to get up again, but she can't. Peter is gripping her ankle like it's a lifeline. She tries to pull herself free, but Peter shakes his head. He points up the stairs.

Karyn follows his finger. She sucks in a huge breath when she sees who's there.

She looks at Peter. Tears run down his cheeks. She wants to wrap him in her arms, tell him everything will be okay.

But nothing is okay. It never will be.

His sobs grow louder. Karyn puts her hands over her ears. She can't stand it anymore. She needs to get out.

Suddenly Peter stands up. Karyn! he shouts, in a voice that's not a voice. It's an explosion. The impact throws her to the ground. Her body slumps to the floor.

CHAPTER THREE

Sunday morning, Karyn rolls out of bed and pulls on her bathrobe. Her head is pounding from a terrible nightmare. She can't piece the entire dream together, but she remembers a cold basement, T. J., Peter Davis. She was running from something. From what?

Karyn shakes the thought from her head and trudges to the kitchen. Once again, there's no coffee brewing. And once again, there's no mom. Karyn doesn't have the energy to get mad. She pulls a coat on over her robe and goes outside for the newspaper.

Back in the kitchen, Karyn makes a cup of tea. After yesterday's tarlike coffee, she figures something herbal is the way to go. She pours herself a bowl of granola, then sits at the kitchen table, flipping through the newspaper. Her favorite part is the travel section. She loves the idea of faraway places. She's always felt like Paris would be her favorite city, if she could ever go there. The sophisticated clothes. Rich foods. And of course, the romance.

On the front page of this week's travel section is an article about bed-and-breakfasts in New England. Not quite Paris, but still romantic. Karyn stares at the photo of a nineteenth-century farmhouse in the middle of a snow-covered meadow. Next to the house is an old-fashioned sleigh filled with dried flowers. Funny, this kind of place is just what she pictures when she fantasizes about losing her virginity.

Karyn puts the paper on the table and gazes into space with a frown. Is she just being crazy, thinking it could really be like that? Does anyone else still believe that sex should be sweet and soft and romantic and beautiful, not just the first time but always? Obviously not her mom. But it couldn't have always been like that for her. When her mom was her age, didn't she fantasize about having sex with a man she loved and then being with him forever?

Yeah, maybe she did, Karyn realizes with a pang of guilt. *And then Dad messed it all up when he left her.* That's scary. There's no way her mom could have predicted that her husband would end up leaving her for some younger woman years down the road, right? Because why would she have married him if she thought it was possible? Even Karyn never would have thought her dad could do that to her mom. To her. Yeah, the fights were bad. But didn't he love Karyn and her mom enough to stick around, to keep trying? How could he give up on them both so easily?

What Karyn has never been able to get, since the

moment her parents told her about the divorce, is how love can end if it's real—unless the person who *used to* love you and stopped just isn't who you thought they were. Isn't strong and loyal enough to fight for you. Like her dad.

But then how can anyone ever know what's right, who they really love and who really loves them? How is she supposed to know when the right time to have sex is, when it's okay to give herself one hundred percent to someone else?

Karyn thinks of the box of condoms sitting in her dresser. Unopened. Unused. She bought them weeks ago. Occasionally she'll pull them out and examine the silhouette of the couple holding hands on the box. She'll even pretend it's her and T. J. in the picture. But that's as far as she gets. *Gemma's right—if that's all the fantasy I can come up with, he's gonna find someone else.*

No. He won't find someone else. I'm the one he loves. T. J. isn't like Karyn's dad—he would never leave her. He makes her feel completely adored, which is her *real* fantasy come true. That's why it's so silly to be afraid to sleep with him. So why can't she let herself imagine it?

She closes her eyes.

Okay, I'm coming back from a long walk with T. J. We go inside, and he lights a fire. We cover ourselves with a blanket. He kisses my neck. Moves his lips down my throat, reaches a hand under my sweater. Wait . . . wait . . . this is wrong. I can't see T. J.'s face. Why can't I see his face?

She opens her eyes and pushes the paper away, frustrated.

Her mom's the one sleeping with random, faceless guys—not her. So what's her problem?

Karyn drums her fingers on the table. The day looms ahead of her, filled with more nothing. Her friends are all busy, and Reed's probably still sick. *He could come over here and finish his work. I could make him some soup.*

Karyn gets up and walks over to the phone. She picks it up and dials the Frasiers' number.

"Hello?"

"Hi, Mrs. Frasier. It's Karyn."

"Hi, Karyn. I've missed seeing you around." Mrs. Frasier has always been good to her—over the years when Karyn was her younger son's best friend, and then especially when she became her older son's girlfriend.

"You must be looking for Reed," Mrs. Frasier says.

"Yep," Karyn replies. "I hope he's feeling okay."

"Reed? He's fine," she says, sounding confused. "Let me get him for you."

Karyn plays with the phone cord while she waits. *He really was sick last night, wasn't he? Of course he was.* It's just like Reed to pretend to his mom that he's fine when he's not. He's definitely not the typical spoiled younger sibling.

"Karyn?"

She smiles at the sound of his voice. "Just checking in. Wanted to see if you were feeling better."

He clears his throat. "Yeah, just a little overtired, I guess. I'm sorry. I hope I didn't ruin your night."

"No way, I spent a romantic evening with Tom Hanks and Meg Ryan," she jokes.

"*You've Got Mail*?"

"Better. *Sleepless in Seattle.*"

"Ohhh, next time I bail, I'll make sure it's a better TV night."

"There won't be a next time, I hope," Karyn says.

Reed chuckles. "Absolutely not. And I promise I will make it up to you."

See, no big deal. Everything is back to normal.

"How about today?" she suggests. "Why don't I make you some chicken soup? I swear you'll feel better."

"You? Make chicken soup?" Reed laughs. "What other talents of yours am I not aware of?"

"Careful. There's lots you don't know about me," Karyn says. "Well, okay, maybe not. But it's not too hard to open a Campbell's can, right?"

"Tempting. But how about the *Godfather* marathon at your place instead? It starts at noon. Ninety minutes until show time."

Karyn's smile widens. "Sounds good, but you'll have to pick up some snacks. No munchies in the house."

"No problem. I'll be over by noon."

"Perfect. See you then."

Karyn hangs up. *Good. A plan.*

She hurries to the bathroom for a shower, relieved to feel the hot water hitting her back and shoulders. She closes her eyes. Soon the picture of the farmhouse returns to her mind. It's surrounded by snow. Miles and miles of white powder. Not a single house in sight. Why can she fantasize about a house in the middle of nowhere, but she can't take being home alone?

Because in the fantasy, she's not alone. There's someone in the farmhouse with her. He's standing behind her, whispering in her ear. *What's he saying?* Karyn concentrates, but she just can't hear the words.

• • •

Reed rummages around on his bedroom floor for his khakis, then puts them on with his favorite green sweater. Usually his room's neater, but it got a little messy when Jeremy was sleeping on the air mattress on his floor. After the first week or two, when it became obvious Jeremy wasn't going home anytime soon, Reed's mom fixed up the guest room for him. But Reed still hasn't gotten his room organized again. He digs under his bed for his Nikes, humming along with the U2 song playing on his stereo.

He's in a pretty good mood, even though he didn't sleep that well. He felt terrible about lying to Karyn.

I'm so glad she called and things are fine. A relaxing day of hanging out in front of the TV is just what he needs.

"Wanna go for a run?" Reed looks up and sees Jeremy standing in the doorway in a T-shirt and sweats.

"No, I'm going over to Karyn's. *Godfather* marathon."

"Haven't you seen all those movies at least twice already?" Jeremy asks.

"Three times," Reed answers. "I'm going for a record. You should stop by after your run."

Jeremy shakes his head. "You know I'm not really into mob movies. Besides, I'm hoping to hook up with Emily. Maybe go get hot chocolate with her again or something."

"That's cool," Reed says. "So your parents still haven't . . . I mean, you haven't talked to them about stuff?"

Jeremy sighs. "My dad hasn't called, no," he says.

Reed feels terrible. He just doesn't know what to say to his friend. Too bad Karyn's not here—she'd know what to tell Jeremy. "Maybe you could try talking to them again," Reed suggests. "If you go over there today?"

"We'll see. Maybe. Say hi to Karyn," Jeremy says. "I'm going for that run."

"Let me know what happens," Reed calls out after him. He grabs his wallet and car keys off his dresser and heads downstairs. He pulls his letterman jacket from the closet, but just as he's about to reach for the doorknob, the phone rings. Reed hesitates. He really just wants to go. But what if it's Karyn? She's probably calling to say she wants him to pick up some obscure food that goes along with her love of Mafia movies. Reed laughs to himself and hurries to pick up the phone.

"Hello?"

"Hey, man, it's your big brother."

Reed's muscles tense.

"How's it going?" Reed asks. Why does he feel like T. J.'s calling to ream him out for going over to Karyn's, when that's obviously ridiculous?

"Okay, I guess. But Coach just told us that the whole team has to stay in town for the Thanksgiving Day game. Even if we're not gonna play. What's the point of all of us warming the bench on a holiday?"

Reed can hear the genuine disappointment in his brother's voice. He carries the phone into the kitchen and sits down. "That's college football for you," Reed says, trying to make it sound like a cool reason to miss Thanksgiving.

"I'm just getting a little sick of these guys' faces, you know." Obviously, T. J. doesn't think it's cool.

"It sucks you won't be here, but you'll probably have more fun with your friends, anyway. Thanksgiving is just an overrated gorge fest." Reed doesn't have much practice making T. J. feel better. It's rare for the guy to ever be upset about anything, especially when it involves football.

"Yeah, but you know, it's *Thanksgiving*."

"Yeah, I know," Reed answers, kicking the leg of the kitchen table.

"But whatever, man. What's one turkey day?" T. J. says.

Reed can tell his brother is really hurting. Words don't come too easily to him, but T. J. doesn't have to say anything else. Reed gets it. Thanksgiving was their father's favorite holiday. Some years they'd have close to thirty people over. Distant cousins, great-great aunts and uncles, half

44

cousins—anyone who might be remotely related—was invited. Each year there was a new face. Mr. Frasier prided himself on keeping his family united. That one day, everyone had to be there together—and nobody could fight.

"I could document the whole thing on video and send it FedEx if you want," Reed says, half serious.

"I'm cool. It's no big deal," T. J. answers. "I'd rather get hammered with the team, anyway."

Reed winces. He hates when T. J. gets into tough guy mode. But he knows it's how T. J. gets through things. It's how he got through everything that happened when they were kids.

I've been complaining that I make all the sacrifices. What am I thinking? So I faked being sick so T. J. wouldn't be taken out of a game. What's one stupid game? T. J. sacrificed his entire childhood for me. If anyone should be complaining, it's him.

"I just hope Karyn will be able to visit me," T. J. says, his tone lightening up.

Reed feels himself being pulled inside out as a swarm of emotions battle for the surface. "Yeah, that'd be cool," he manages to say.

"When are you gonna come by, little brother? Wouldn't want you heading off to college without some practice at a frat party."

"Maybe after the holidays," Reed answers vaguely.

"So, you got plans today?" T. J. asks.

Reed stares across the room at the magnets on the

fridge. "Uh . . . not really. Just meeting Bobby Scorella for lunch. Maybe catch a movie." Why is he lying?

"Okay, man. Break the news to Mom gently," T. J. says.

"Sure thing. Talk to ya soon."

"Bye."

Reed hangs up, then drops his head into his palm. *Good. Now you've lied to both T. J. and Karyn in less than twenty-four hours.*

• • •

Late Sunday morning, Peter wheels himself across a shiny tile floor. The room he's in resembles a small gymnasium. Complicated contraptions fitted with pulleys, sliding seats, and a whole array of strange mechanisms are scattered around. There's also a big blue mat and a large net filled with colorful balls. *Like an adult playroom,* Peter thinks. Peter's been on the waiting list for this clinic ever since the accident. It specializes in spinal cord injuries and is supposedly the best in the Northeast.

He's following Dr. Ed Watson—Ed, as he's been instructed to call the surprisingly tall doctor—to the other side of the room. Ed is young, probably in his mid-thirties. Everything about him is big. Big hands, big feet, big features. He's got to be at least seven feet tall. Gigantic. At least that's how it looks to Peter, who's lost about half of his standing height from being confined to a wheelchair.

They pass a middle-aged man whose legs are hooked through some sort of pulley device. A doctor moves the

46

pulley back and forth, causing the guy's legs to move. The two are laughing about something. Peter can't comprehend laughter in a place like this.

On the blue mat is a young girl, about ten or eleven. Her blond hair is tied back in a long ponytail. Her doctor is helping her sit on top of a blue rubber ball. It seems pretty easy, but she keeps rolling off. "Balance and focus. Balance and focus," her doctor keeps repeating. She catches Peter staring and he quickly looks away.

It's not fair. What did that kid ever do? She shouldn't have to spend her time here learning how to sit on some stupid ball.

Peter's nervous. Nervous because he doesn't know what to expect. Nervous because therapy might not work. He might never regain the use of his legs.

And why should I, when that poor girl is stuck here? There's no way she deserves it—no way she did anything like what Peter did when he was her age. And he knows, deep down, that that's why he's here today. It's why the drunk driver hit him. He was finally being punished for having done the unthinkable all those years ago.

"Well, Peter, it's our first day," Ed says when they reach a far corner of the room. "We'll start with warm-ups."

Next to them is a low cushioned table about six feet long. Ed leans in close to help Peter onto the table. He slides his hands underneath Peter, but Peter shrinks away, embarrassed by his weakness. He's sick of being handled by everyone. Before the accident, he barely touched anyone.

47

Now every insignificant maneuver means coming in contact with another human.

"You're going to have to work with me, Peter," Ed says. "We'll get a routine down soon enough and you won't even need me."

Peter takes a deep breath. All week his feelings about this appointment have been a mixture of anticipation and fear. His parents have been so excited for him to start therapy. Therapy means rehabilitation. Rehabilitation means his legs are going to have a purpose again. What they don't know is that this is his fate. He's been trying not to face it, but he can't avoid it much longer.

"Listen," Ed says. "I've seen a lot of people go through the same thing you are. And I've spent a lot of time in physical therapy myself. Blew out a knee during a basketball game and the doctors predicted I'd walk with a cane for the rest of my life. But I worked it out. It can happen."

Peter inhales deeply. *I'd take a strut like Frankenstein if it meant I could be on my feet again.*

"I'm all yours," Peter says.

Together they maneuver Peter up onto the table. He lies on his back, staring at the soft light overhead. *Please, please let this work. Please let me feel something.*

"I'm going to put my hand behind your knee and bend it back and forth," Ed says.

Peter nods. He keeps his eyes focused on the light. Afraid to look. He knows what he'll see. Something that resembles a leg. But not his leg. Just some strange appendage that happens to be attached to his body.

"You should watch," Ed suggests. "It helps to connect the physical and the mental."

Peter looks in the direction of his legs. Ed has one hand behind his knee and the other at the base of his foot. Slowly Ed pushes his left knee back and forth toward his chest. Peter feels nothing. They do this for a while, alternating between legs. The monotony of the exercise is pretty ridiculous. What's the point? This guy can pump his legs all he wants; it's not gonna make Peter feel anything.

"Everything okay?" Ed asks.

Peter shrugs. He's tired. Bored.

"Okay, now it's time for you to do some work," Ed says.

What do you suggest? A sprint?

Peter watches as Ed walks over to a weight rack and picks up two ten-pound dumbbells. He hands them to Peter.

"If you hadn't noticed, my legs are in worse shape than my arms," Peter says sarcastically.

"Thanks for the info." Ed chuckles. "But if you don't have upper body strength, you'll never be able to help the lower half along. I want you to hold these above your chest and press. Use the strength in your chest and your upper arms. Start with three sets of fifteen."

Peter takes the weights from Ed. He holds them over his chest as Ed instructed. Ten pounds, big deal. *This is lame.*

I'm gonna tell my parents this fancy clinic idea of theirs is a waste of time.

Peter squeezes his muscles together and straightens his arms once, twice, three times. A slight strain spreads across his upper body. Lifting is harder than he thought. By fifteen, a layer of sweat has broken out on his upper lip.

"Easy?" Ed asks with a smirk.

"No problem," Peter replies, trying to stifle a gasp. He starts the second set. By the time he reaches the eighth repetition, the sweat is running down the sides of his face. His muscles are on fire. He has no idea how he's going to finish the next seven, let alone another set.

"Come on Peter, just a few more," Ed encourages.

Peter can't believe it. He's exhausted. But the adrenaline pumping through his veins helps him finish the third set. He lets out a groan. *When was the last time I had an adrenaline rush?*

"It'll feel worse tomorrow," Ed says.

"Great. I can't wait." His tone is sarcastic, but inside, Peter knows it's the truth. He *can't* wait for the pain. For so long, he's felt like a steel wall separated his body from his mind. It's a relief to see they're still connected.

"So is there a weight room at school you can use?" Ed asks. "Because you should really practice these exercises at least every other day."

"Yeah, there's one in the gym," Peter says. "I guess I can use it."

Peter looks across the room and sees the little blond girl sitting in a chair, tossing the ball back and forth with her doctor. She's smiling, looking hopeful. Looking how he felt when he lifted those weights just now.

And it occurs to him. If she's not here because she did something wrong—then maybe, just maybe, neither is he.

• • •

Karyn and Reed sit side by side in the Aufieros' family room, watching *The Godfather*. On the coffee table in front of them is an almost empty bowl of popcorn and two Cokes. *This is definitely the right way to spend a Sunday afternoon,* Karyn thinks as she hugs a throw pillow to her chest.

And Reed seems perfectly happy to zone out in front of the TV. Yesterday's grouchiness was probably just because he wasn't feeling well. Karyn looks at the clock. Her mom had called a little while ago, saying she was meeting some friends for brunch. She didn't mention their fight last night or the fact that she hadn't come home.

Brunch. Yeah, right. Karyn doesn't even want to imagine where her mom really is. She gets that her mom is lonely. But *she's* lonely, too, sometimes, and she doesn't run out and have sex with someone because of it. She just invites her best friend over to watch movies on TV.

Karyn turns to look at Reed's profile. He's spaced out on a commercial for a bathroom cleaner. For once, he's not wearing his ever-present baseball cap. She's never noticed that his eyebrows are a little darker than his hair. Well, of course she's noticed, but not really. Whenever she sees Reed, she sees the person she's been friends with for her whole life—not the details of what he looks like.

She examines his features more closely. His defined jawbone. The pronounced chin. A sprinkling of stubble, red like his hair, but a little lighter. And soft. Not that Karyn has touched it, but she can just tell by looking.

Karyn hugs her pillow tighter. Reed's definitely quieter than usual today. Maybe he's still not feeling well. She watches him rub his chin with his long fingers. He and T. J. are unmistakably brothers, but at the same time their faces are different. Their expressions, maybe. And Reed's face is more chiseled, his jaw a little more defined.

What's wrong with you? Why are you staring at him?

She blinks, then shifts her attention back to the television. A shampoo commercial. She forces herself to focus on the smiling woman lathering up in the shower.

Finally the movie comes on again, but Reed leans forward and rubs his temples.

"Please tell me the movie is making you tired and not me," she says.

"It's not you," he says with a faint smile. "I guess I'm still not feeling great."

"Anything I can do?" she asks.

He squints. "You know those headaches you get right behind your eyes?"

Karyn tilts her head in sympathy. "Those are the worst."

"Yeah," he says, his muscular frame sinking low into the couch.

"I know just the cure. Sit up."

Reed obeys and Karyn moves closer. *What are you doing? You so don't know a cure.* But the words had just come out, and they felt right somehow.

"Okay," she says. "Relax and close your eyes." Gently she rubs her hands together, generating some warmth between her palms. Then she reaches forward and places her fingers on his temples. The heat of his skin is electric, and all at once, the world around her stops moving. She's never felt anything like this.

What's going on? This is Reed.

But her body doesn't seem to get that. Her heart is suddenly racing, and every nerve is alert. Still, even through the dizziness, it feels so natural to touch him. It's like she knows exactly how to make him feel better, exactly how much pressure her fingers need to apply.

A tightness forms in her stomach. A combination of fear and excitement, emotions that don't make any sense right now, but somehow do in a way she can't understand.

Something tells her this is wrong. She shouldn't be touching Reed, not if it makes her feel like this. But it's just the two of them in this room, and all she knows is she doesn't want this sensation to end.

53

"Just imagine you're somewhere peaceful," Karyn murmurs. "Like—like a quiet farmhouse in Vermont." She slides her hands from his temples to his scalp.

"Mmm . . . a quiet farmhouse in the winter with a frozen lake nearby," Reed adds softly. "And maybe a hill for sledding."

She moves her fingers through his hair, wondering if he can hear her heart thumping wildly in her chest.

"Then there's gotta be a warm kitchen for all the hot chocolate afterward," Reed goes on. "And a fireplace to lie in front of."

The tightness in Karyn's stomach begins to spread. She breathes slowly, trying to relax. She can't seem to get her pulse to slow down. She also can't pretend that Reed has not just described her fantasy, as if he's been inside her head. She continues to massage his temples, examining the delicate skin around his eyes. Her gaze rests on the tiny half-moon-shaped scar above his left eyebrow, the one he got from falling off his bike when he was eight.

Every scar he has, every mark he got growing up, is a part of her past, her history. She stares at his face, his familiar soft smile, and then closes her eyes and is back in that farmhouse, by the roaring fire. The hands on her shoulders, the lips on her neck—

Her eyes snap open. They're Reed's hands. Reed's lips. *Reed's* face is the one in her fantasy, not T. J.'s.

No. I can't be thinking this.

Reed opens his eyes and meets her gaze, but he looks as lost as she feels right now.

She stops moving her fingers. *Yes. He's the one in my fantasy. And he has been all along, hasn't he? It's crazy, I know. But somehow it's not. That's why I could never really see his face or hear his voice.*

Karyn holds her breath. She traces Reed's cheek with her thumb. Her hands tremble. Slowly she slides her thumb closer to his bottom lip. Reed doesn't stop her.

No rules. He is the person in my fantasy. Reed.

Her throat tightens. *No rules now, but what happens later? What happens when I see T. J.? How do I look at him, tell him I'm . . . I'm what?*

In love with Reed.

It's true. In that second, she's more certain of it than she's ever been of anything in her life. It's not just Reed's scars that she knows as well as her own—it's everything about him. His favorite songs, movies, TV shows. The fact that he'll only eat nachos with gobs of sour cream and can't stand tomatoes unless they're in pasta sauce or ketchup. How scared he is of spiders, even though he'd never admit it to anyone else. The way his eyes light up at the mere mention of snow in the forecast because winter isn't winter until he and Karyn have made snow angels in the park near his house.

And it's the same with her—Reed knows every detail about who she is, what she's been through, how she thinks. He's the one she called when she actually got an A on a math test for the first—and only—time ever. He was at her side the day her dad moved out of the house, and he was the only person she let see her cry during the divorce.

It's unbelievable that she didn't know it before—a month ago, a week ago, or even ten *minutes* ago. Because hasn't she always loved him? Unless that's exactly why she couldn't see it for so long.

Karyn knows she should stop. Turn around. Watch the television. But she can't ignore what's happening inside her, what's happening between her and Reed. She can't.

Reed's eyes are locked on hers, mirroring back all of the longing, the desire, that she feels. Slowly she leans forward. *No rules . . .*

She shuts her eyes, smells his skin. *I can't believe I'm about to do this. . . .*

Their lips meet. Gently at first. Cautious. A rush of emotion whips through her body. Spinning, spinning . . . Karyn is lost in his lips. Nothing distracts her. Not the noise from the television. Not even the thought of T. J.

She feels Reed's hand touch her lower back and lets out a small sigh. Her palm cradles his cheek, and she presses her lips harder against his. The spinning speeds up until she feels like she's going to explode. It's an incredible feeling. Like a dam has been destroyed. Pure freedom.

Suddenly she feels his body stiffen. Gunshots sound from the television, and Reed pushes her away, wiping at his mouth.

He stares at her in shock. "What was that?" he demands. "What were you thinking?"

Karyn blinks. *Thinking? I wasn't thinking.* "I—I don't know," she stammers, looking down at her open palm. She balls it into a tight fist.

What has she done? She's kissed Reed.

Reed stands up and begins to pace back and forth in front of the TV. He's holding both hands in front of him like he doesn't know where they belong.

"Reed, I—it just—didn't you feel it, too?"

He stops and looks at her, and she honestly can *feel* her heart break. The pain in his eyes . . . it's like she's just torn some essential body part right out of him.

Karyn swallows a sob. "I'm sorry . . . I shouldn't have."

Reed shakes his head. "No. No. That shouldn't have happened. Definitely shouldn't have . . ." His voice trails off and he starts pacing again. All the color has drained from his face.

She has no idea what to say, no clue what he's feeling right now. In a way, he almost seems more *scared* than angry, but it doesn't make any sense. What's he afraid of? T. J.? Reed wasn't the one who did this—*she* kissed *him.*

"It's my fault," she says. "I just thought . . . I thought you wanted it, too."

"Why would you think that?" Reed snaps.

She flinches, tears coming to her eyes. Had she imagined what she'd seen in his face right before they kissed?

Had she imagined his hand pressing her closer? "Didn't you feel it, too?" she squeaks out.

Silence. Karyn holds her breath. He turns away so he's facing the television. *Why won't he look at me?*

"I was kissing a beautiful girl, Karyn," he says, his voice distant, foreign. "I'm a guy. What do you expect?" He moves so he's looking in her direction again but still not facing her. "But I'm just wondering—did you completely forget about your boyfriend? About my *brother*, T. J.?"

An emptiness wells up inside her at his tone, more terrifying than any loneliness she's ever felt before. Reed hates her. She has just realized that she loves him, and in the same moment she's made him hate her. And then a truly horrible thought hits her. *I'm as bad as my mom. No, worse. Even she would never do this—would never cheat on someone with his own brother.*

"Please go," she says.

He looks at her, his expression losing some of its coldness. The pain and confusion return to his eyes. He stuffs his hands into the front pockets of his pants, shifting awkwardly. "Look, Karyn. It's just—this was a mistake. A serious mistake, and I—"

"I said go!" she interrupts.

Finally he turns to leave. As his footsteps fade down the hall, her shoulders convulse and the tears stream down her face.

CHAPTER FOUR

How could I *let this happen? How could I ruin an entire friendship in five seconds?* Karyn rolls over on her side and stares out the window. The sky is darker than usual for three o'clock. Next to her is a pile of crumpled tissues. Karyn's head hurts from crying. All she can do is replay the scene over and over in her mind, but it never makes any more sense. It's like it wasn't even her leaning in for the kiss. Someone else massaged Reed's temples. Someone else touched his cheeks, his lips. Someone else cheated on T. J.

Down the hall, she hears her mother in her bedroom. Ms. Aufiero arrived a little after Reed left and knocked on Karyn's door, but Karyn had pretended to be taking a nap. The last thing she'd needed was to come face-to-face with a reminder of everything she hates, everything she never wanted to be, but is well on the road toward becoming.

Karyn reaches up and touches the puffiness around her eyes. She can't leave her room until the swelling has gone down. No way is she going to tell her mother what happened.

Or tell anyone, for that matter. She flips onto her back. She can still feel Reed's lips on her own. She remembers how much she'd felt for him, how her thoughts had all blended together into one overwhelming need to kiss him. At that moment, she'd been so convinced that it was the right thing to do, that Reed was the one she wanted. But now, lying here alone in her room, she has no idea what she really wants.

What if it was just one of those crazy moments where her brain had tricked her, because she was lonely and missed T. J.? Reed has been her friend for years—wouldn't she have known it if she was in love with him?

She loves T. J., doesn't she? How could she not? He's devoted, and sweet, and gorgeous—and he treats her like a princess. He's what every girl wants, and she's so happy when she's with him. A different kind of happy than when she and Reed hang out, but isn't that why it makes sense for T. J. to be her boyfriend, not Reed? Yes, she and Reed know everything about each other—but does that really mean they're meant to be more than friends, or instead that they're *better* as friends?

Karyn swipes away the crumpled tissues in a surge of disgust. She hates herself for being so weak. So lonely that she would talk herself into believing she's in love with her friend and then throw herself at him.

And then be rejected.

Karyn looks at the photo on her nightstand of her and T. J. Last summer they'd driven to New York City, their first weekend away together. Someone had taken their picture on the Brooklyn Bridge with the Statue of Liberty in the background. The day had been perfect. Sunny, but not too hot. They walked for miles, then he'd taken her to an expensive restaurant and bought her a rose from a man selling flowers outside the restaurant.

More tears well up behind her eyes. After he gave her the rose, he'd said, "I love you," for the first time.

Karyn picks up the phone. *I just need to hear his voice. Then I'll know. I'll know it's T. J. I love, not Reed.*

The phone rings. Karyn holds her breath, a small part of her afraid that he'll just be able to know in some psychic way that she kissed his brother.

"Hello?"

"Hey, Teej." *Try and sound normal.*

"Hey, babe. I was just about to call you. God, I miss you so much."

It feels like her heart's being put through a shredder. It's been torn in so many pieces today, she can't believe she's even still breathing at all.

"I was just looking at that picture of us in New York City last summer," she says, wiping leftover tears from her face.

"Which picture?"

Karyn swallows. "You know, the one where we're on the Brooklyn Bridge. The Statue of Liberty is behind us."

"Brooklyn Bridge . . ." T. J.'s voice trails off.

Karyn stands up and walks over to her dresser. She

stares at herself in the mirror and frowns. "We took it after we walked all the way down to the Seaport and ate sushi."

"Ugh! That's right. That was definitely one of the grossest meals of my life."

"Oh, I didn't know you hated it so much," Karyn says.

"You know me. I'm all meat and potatoes." He pauses. "But it's not like I cared, since I was too busy being psyched that I was there with you," he adds.

It's the kind of thing that normally turns her to mush. But somehow right now—she feels nothing. And suddenly she realizes that calling T. J. was the wrong idea. She had wanted the reassurance of T. J.'s voice. Wanted everything to be like it was yesterday. But one phone call is not going to make that happen. If she has to say another word, she's going to burst into tears. "Um, Teej, my mom is calling me, so I've gotta go," she says weakly.

"Oh, okay," he says, obviously disappointed. "But hey, wait—there's something I want to ask you."

"Uh-huh?"

"I'm stuck up here for Thanksgiving, and I was wondering if you wanted to be stuck up here with me?"

Thanksgiving. Right.

"You there?"

"Yeah, T. J., I'm here," she manages.

"So what do you say?"

Yes. Just say yes.

But her mouth won't listen to her mind. If only it had

worked that way earlier. "I'll have to check with my mom," she tells him. "You know, it's her first holiday without Dad around."

"Oh yeah," he says. "That's right, I forgot. But if you could try to convince her—I just really want to see you."

"I'll . . . um . . . I'll try," she promises.

"I love you."

Say it back. "I . . . love you . . . too, T. J."

• • •

"Yo, Reed, you on another planet or something?"

Reed looks up at Rory Pantalone, the assistant manager at TCBY, then tries not to cringe. Rory's a chain smoker and he reeks of tobacco. "Just a little distracted, I guess. Sorry."

Rory is obviously referring to Reed's third mistake of the evening, ringing up one hundred dollars instead of ten on the cash register.

Of course, "distracted" doesn't quite sum up Reed's emotions at the moment. More like shell-shocked. And that's just the tip of the iceberg.

"Well, I need to head home early," Rory says. "I want to make sure you and Jane can handle things."

No matter how far away Reed stands, he can still smell Rory's breath. "Sure, Rory. We've locked up a million times."

Two teenage girls burst through the door. Their high-pitched laughter is enough to make Reed's already frazzled nerves snap completely.

"Dude, they're all yours," Rory says, then heads through the back to the manager's office.

"Excuse me," one of the girls, a tall blond, says loudly. "Can I get a vanilla cone with sprinkles?"

Reed glances at Jane, who's working the other end of the counter. They exchange helpless smiles.

"Sure," he says to the girl, putting on a fake smile.

Reed stands next to the yogurt machine, watching the vanilla swirl onto the cone. It's been hours since he left Karyn's house. Hours since they kissed. Correction. Since *she* kissed *him*. That's what happened, right? Yeah, he's been going a little crazy inside with his attraction to Karyn lately, but he'd thought he was doing a pretty good job of keeping all that hidden. So then what made her kiss him? How did she know it was what he wanted—*everything* he wanted?

I don't believe it actually happened. What was I thinking? I wasn't. My brain totally froze from the moment I felt her fingers on my forehead. Except, that isn't exactly true, either. Because he can remember one thought as she massaged his head, one thought that only grew stronger as they kissed. He remembers realizing that as much as he knew before then that he wanted Karyn, that he was crazy about her, it was suddenly clear how major his feelings for her really are. He remembers knowing in every inch of his being that he is completely, ridiculously in love with her.

"Are you going to give me my cone?"

Reed turns around, flustered. "Oh yeah. Here. Sorry about that," he mutters, handing it to her.

"Can I have a peanut butter cone?" the other girl asks. She's got curly brown hair. Blue eyes. Blue with flecks of gold. Karyn's eyes. She's even got the same long lashes, the same wide-eyed stare.

"Is there a problem?" the girl asks.

Reed shakes his head and grabs another cone. *Pull yourself together. You're gonna freak people out.*

He holds the cone under the yogurt machine. How many times has he looked into Karyn's eyes? Probably more times than he's looked into anyone else's on this planet. But this afternoon was different. Today her eyes were so close to his, closer than ever.

Stop. She's not your girlfriend. And you're not her boyfriend. Which is exactly why she shouldn't have kissed you.

Why did she say she thought I felt it, too? How did she know?

Reed gives the peanut butter cone to the girl, avoiding eye contact. He's never felt as sleazy as he did standing there in Karyn's den, telling her that he'd kissed her back because she was pretty, same as he'd do with any pretty girl. He saw what he was doing to her, and it crushed him. But it would have been far worse to admit the truth, to tell her just how life-altering that kiss had been. Because then he wouldn't just be the guy whose brother's girlfriend kissed him. He'd be the guy who wanted it to happen, who *let* it happen. Maybe Karyn could live with betraying T. J., but there's no way Reed could.

"Are you okay?" Jane asks, coming up next to him.

65

"A little out of it," he admits, raking a hand through his hair. "But better now that the customers are gone."

"Don't tell me it's your turn to pass out. I don't think I can handle the store by myself."

"No, I'll be fine," Reed says with a smile. "Hey, did you ever figure out why that happened, by the way? Did you see a doctor?" Jane was in seriously bad shape last time they were here. He'd practically had to carry her to his car to get her home.

"No, I think it was just—just stress," Jane says, rubbing her forehead.

Reed raises his eyebrows. "Wow, so the mighty Jane Scott actually *does* feel pressure? I'm amazed. You know, you've been busting your butt for four years. I think you can afford to go a little easy on yourself now. Especially since things will only get rougher when you're at Harvard or Yale in the fall."

Jane winces, then looks at him with a strange, unusually vulnerable look in her brown eyes. "I should probably tell you," she says.

Reed frowns. "Tell me what?"

She twirls the tie on her apron around her fingers. "I haven't told anyone. Well, just my parents. But the truth has to come out sooner or later."

Reed gives her an encouraging nod, puzzled.

"It's about Harvard and Yale," she says softly.

"Don't tell me, you got into both? Of course you did. How did you find out already?"

Jane lets out a harsh laugh. "Reed, there's no way I'm getting into Harvard or Yale. In fact, right now I wouldn't even have a chance at a state school."

Reed just stares at her, totally confused.

"You know how I've been saying that my SAT scores haven't come yet?" she begins, running her hands along the counter. He notices she's carefully avoiding his gaze.

"Yeah, I figured you've been sparing us the humiliation. But that's . . . that's not it, is it?"

Jane presses her lips together. "I wish." She pauses, takes a deep breath. "Reed, I couldn't even answer a question. I lost it. I had a total breakdown."

Reed's eyes widen. "What do you mean?"

"I mean I freaked. Went blank. My brain turned to static." She grabs a napkin from the dispenser and starts brushing a few scattered cookie crumbs and nuts from the counter. "I got the points for signing my name, and that's it."

"Oh, man, I feel like such a jerk," Reed says. "I shouldn't have kept bugging you about your scores like that. It must have been the last thing you needed. I—I had no idea."

"No one did. I finally told my parents Friday night," Jane says.

"You know, you can still take them again," Reed suggests.

Jane sighs. "Now you sound like my parents."

"Sorry. God, I don't know what to say. I'm sure you'll figure it out. You're the smartest person I know, by a long shot." He gives her shoulder an encouraging squeeze, but he's still too shocked by the fact that Jane Scott actually messed something up to offer any real advice. It's like the whole universe got whacked out of alignment today. He doesn't think he can process much more. Actually, he hasn't processed much of anything that's happened today since the moment Karyn's lips touched his.

The bell over the door jingles, and Reed glances up to see who's coming in. But it's just Jane's dad, not a customer. Good. He's not sure he's got the mental capabilities right now to even ring up a simple order.

Reed looks back at Jane, noticing that she doesn't look nearly as relieved to see her father.

• • •

Jane stares at her dad, frozen to the spot. He's here, in TCBY. He's here to see her. And she has no idea what to expect.

She hasn't seen him since Friday night, since she showed him her SAT scores and he totally lost it on her. But he's had some time to calm down now, to accept the truth. Which means . . . ?

"Dad," she finally says, her voice coming out a little rusty. She clears her throat.

"Hello, Jane," he responds. "Do you have a minute?"

Jane looks around the empty store.

"You don't look too busy," Mr. Scott says, without a trace of irony.

Jane notices the pointed white collar of her father's shirt. Even on a Sunday, he's dressed for work. He never takes a break. "Just interrupt me if you need anything," she tells Reed.

She takes in a quick breath, then walks over to her father. At first, after she shoved those scores in her parents' faces Friday night, she felt an incredible freedom. The tight coil of tension that was always wrapped around her, pushing her to keep going and doing, doing, doing—it had disappeared. But over the course of the weekend it's come back, bit by bit, as she's realized what she still has to face. She already knows her mother isn't ready to stop dreaming of her daughter, the professional musician. So what are the chances her dad really heard what she said on Friday?

"So . . . you wanted to talk to me?" Jane prompts, looking up at her dad's face, which is as unreadable as ever.

"Yes, I—I wanted to—" He stops, looking back at her for a second. Then he reaches out, awkwardly, and folds her into a hug.

Not knowing what else to do, Jane hugs him back. His shirt smells like it just came from the dry cleaner. He squeezes tighter, then finally pulls back. She realizes her hands are shaking.

"Jane, you know I love you, right?" he asks.

Jane smiles nervously. "Yeah, of course." Well, as long as she's Jane Scott, perfect daughter, at least.

"Jane, I want to apologize for the other night," he says.

"Your mother and I—we were caught off guard with your—with what you showed us, and we came down pretty hard on you. But you have to understand, it's only because you're so gifted and I just want to see you succeed to your full potential."

Jane nods. "I know," she says.

"But I understand now, I see how much pressure you must have felt. Is that why you . . . ?" Like her mother, he stops short of asking her outright what happened at the SATs. Are they too scared to really hear the answer? "Well, we can discuss that more later," he says quickly. "For now, we need to focus on where we go from here." He takes her elbow and guides her to a nearby table. They sit down.

Where we go from here. Jane looks at him expectantly, hoping he'll be able to tell her what she hasn't managed to figure out.

"I've checked about a retest," Mr. Scott begins. "You can take the SATs again, no problem. It'll make your applications late, but the schools will accept them. With your grades, I'm sure you won't have a problem."

Jane looks at her lap. Retaking the SATs has always been an option. But the memory of that gymnasium makes the little hairs on her arms stand on end. The bright lights. The rows and rows of desks. And all the students scribbling away. Jane flinches as she remembers the persistent scratch of the pencils filling in those tiny bubbles on the answer sheets. She froze. Sat there freaking out, staring at the words in her booklet. The letters were all jumbled. Senseless.

"You'll need to study, of course," her father continues.

Jane's barely listening. Whenever she thinks back to the test day, her mind gets trapped. *I can't do it again. The same thing will happen.*

"A course will take time," her father is saying, "which is why I think you should take a break from the sax. Drop out of the volunteer orchestra. You don't even get credit for that. You'll still have Academic Decathlon, French club, and the Web site. That's all the Ivy Leagues are interested in, anyway."

Jane sits back in her chair. What did he just say? Drop sax? Drop out of the volunteer band? *I can finally see why he and Mom once got along. They look at things the same way—they both think I can just give up what matters to the other. Neither of them remembers to ask what matters to me.*

Mr. Scott leans forward with a smile. So happy with himself. *How come everything in my life has come down to what college I go to? Why can't he see that an Ivy League school is not an option? Can't he keep loving a daughter who doesn't go to Harvard?*

A few customers walk in and Jane looks to see how Reed's doing. She catches his eye and he winks. It was such a relief telling him the truth about her scores. Somehow she'd been sure that once he, and Sumit, and everyone else at school knew, they'd all think she wasn't who they thought. And sure, Reed was obviously surprised. But it hasn't seemed to change the way he sees her.

The bell jingles, and Jane glances at the door. And nearly has a heart attack.

"Mom?"

Mr. Scott whips his head around. Jane looks back and forth between her parents. *I can't believe this is happening.* She jumps up, filled with a rush of nervous energy. She doesn't want her mom to come any closer. After her parents' marathon fight the other night, anything could happen here. And she can't handle it now. Not in front of strangers or in front of *Reed*.

"Jane, aren't you supposed to be working?" her mother says, her eyes fixed on Mr. Scott.

"I'm taking a break," Jane replies, feeling beads of sweat form around her hairline. "Dad just stopped by to talk about some stuff."

"Oh, I'm sure he did." Her mom's tone is sharp, absolute ice. *Please don't cause a scene. Please.*

"Larissa, I don't think your daughter appreciates your tone in her place of employment," Mr. Scott snaps.

"What tone would that be, Robert?"

"All you need to do is listen to yourself," he says, thrusting his hands up in the air.

No, no, please stop.

"I certainly hope you're not encouraging her to quit music," her mother hisses.

72

"Oh, for heaven's sake," her father says, taking a step closer. "Let's not do this now. We'll just make Jane upset."

They don't care about me. They just care about their stupid plans.

"You didn't seem so concerned about Jane the other night when you were shouting at the top of your lungs."

Jane kneads the muscles in the back of her neck. She can do this. She can be strong. Look what she's already done in the past three days. "Please leave," she says, keeping her voice calm and firm.

But nobody is listening.

"Give me a break, Larissa," Mr. Scott continues. "Your temper has always been unmanageable."

"I said, *please leave*." Jane repeats herself, this time more forcefully.

Both of her parents turn their attention to her, their gazes softening. "Sweetie, I . . . ," her mother starts.

"I don't want to hear it. I'm working." Jane looks at a crack in the floor.

"Larissa," her father says. "Would you mind letting me and Jane finish our conversation?"

"No. We're done," Jane says, summoning all her courage. She looks him in the eye. "I don't want to talk about college or retests or which activities to drop. I need to get back to work."

Mr. Scott's brow furrows in an angry frown. "This retest

is important, Jane. It's the only thing that will help you out of this mess."

This mess. Is that how you see my life?

"Would you let it go already, Robert?" her mom says. "You're the one who's *made* the mess."

"Go!" Jane shouts, louder than intended. The adrenaline is pumping through her veins, giving her energy she didn't know she had. Her body tingles with a mixture of exhilaration and shock. For the second time in her life, she's stood up to her parents. And the weirdest part is it's actually so much easier than trying to be their perfect daughter.

• • •

Karyn stands in her bedroom doorway Sunday evening, her gaze flicking back and forth between her mom's stunned expression and the small dark blue box Ms. Aufiero is holding in her hands. A small blue box Karyn is—*was*—keeping carefully hidden in the bottom of her dresser drawer.

"What are you doing with these?" Ms. Aufiero finally demands.

Karyn starts to answer, then stops when no words come. She looks at the open drawer next to her mother and says the only thing she can think of. "What are you doing looking in my dresser?"

"I was looking for . . . I needed—" Her mother breaks off, letting out a huff of exasperation. "That's not the point," she says, gripping the box more tightly, pointing it at Karyn. "Karyn. Are you having sex?"

74

Karyn scratches the top of her head. She takes in her mom's pink cotton bathrobe, the one she only wears for afternoon naps. Obviously her mom didn't get much sleep last night or probably Friday night, either.

Karyn snorts. She walks over to her mother, takes the box of condoms from her hands, and tosses it onto her bed. She'd thought she was done crying for the day, but she can feel fresh tears coming. Those condoms were for her and T. J., but she hadn't gotten up the guts to use them. And now what's going to happen? And what if—what if the real reason she hadn't brought that box out of its hiding place was because Reed really was the guy she'd wanted to lose her virginity to all along, not T. J.?

"Karyn, you always said you'd come to me if you were going to—" Her mom stops, shakes her head, pulls at her hair. The I'm-at-a-loss movement. Karyn knows because she's caught herself doing the same thing. "God, honey, condoms can break. This is not a game. You're too young!"

Karyn's temper flares. "I thought age didn't matter," she snaps. "I mean, you don't think you're too *old* to run around in miniskirts and spend the night with random guys, right?"

Ms. Aufiero steps back as if she's been slapped, and her eyes shine with tears. "I understand you're upset," she says in a low, strained voice. "But that does not give you the right to talk to me that way. You are my daughter, and I want to know if you're having sex."

Karyn doesn't know whether to cry or scream. It's all blending together . . . the condoms, her hypocritical mother, T. J., Reed—her hypocritical self. How could she kiss T. J.'s own brother when she had a box of condoms upstairs in her bedroom being saved for T. J.? What's wrong with her?

"You can't just disappear for the entire weekend and then expect me to tell you about my private life," Karyn says. "I should be asking who *you're* having sex with."

"I'm a grown woman," Ms. Aufiero insists, folding her arms in front of her chest. "You're still a teenager, no matter how mature you are for your age. And sex is a very complex, very intense step that needs to be taken seriously, especially by someone your age. Now, answer me—are you having sex?"

Karyn takes a deep breath, realizing she doesn't have the energy to keep avoiding the question. Maybe if she gives her mom what she wants, she'll leave her alone. And then Karyn won't have to think about sex, about condoms, about who she really loves.

"No. I'm not," she admits, plopping down on her bed. She brushes a few blond strands out of her face. "I mean I—I haven't. Not yet."

Her mother's whole expression relaxes in relief. She even smiles, a small smile. "I'm so glad to hear that," she says. "So then the condoms, you have them just . . ."

"In case," Karyn supplies for her. *In case I stop being such an idiot and figure out who I'm really in love with, for starters.*

Ms. Aufiero walks into the room and sits down next to her on the bed. "Honey, I realize you and T. J. really *like* each other, but how well do you actually know him? You haven't been together all that long, and he's up in Boston a lot of the time. . . ."

"And how well do you know the men you sleep with?" The words slip out of Karyn's mouth before she's had a chance to realize they're coming.

Her mother flinches but holds Karyn's gaze. "I haven't always made the best choices in my life," she says evenly. "But I love you more than anything in this world, and I'll do whatever I can to keep you from hurting the way I have."

Karyn blinks, trying to hold back the waterfall that's threatening to overflow. She glances over at the condom box, looking at the silhouette of the couple holding hands. They're obviously supposed to be in love. She always thought sex meant love. At least, she hoped sex meant love. But everything she's seen her mom do since the divorce, and now even her own thoughts and actions with T. J. and Reed . . . what if she really was just being naive?

"I'm sorry if I haven't set a very good example," Ms. Aufiero continues softly. "I'm so, so sorry," she adds, her voice cracking. Karyn turns back to her and sees the tears spilling down her mother's cheeks.

"No, Mom, I—I'm sorry," Karyn says in a rush. She can't stand to see her mother cry.

Ms. Aufiero leans over and wraps her arms around Karyn, holding her so tightly, Karyn can barely breathe. "I love you so much, sweetie," she murmurs into Karyn's hair.

"I know," Karyn says, returning the hug.

Her mom pulls back slightly, looking into Karyn's eyes. Her face is blotchy from crying, but she's smiling. "What if we have a girls' night tonight, just you and me? We could make a special dinner together."

Karyn looks at her hopefully. "Really?"

Ms. Aufiero nods.

"But I thought you were going out with Nora and Meg tonight."

"That's not until later," her mom explains. "How about tossing together some chicken fajitas?"

Karyn pauses. Did she actually get through to her mother, finally? Is it too much to hope that one good thing could come from this nightmare of a day?

"Yeah, fajitas sound great," she says with a weak smile.

CHAPTER FiVE

Monday morning, Karyn wakes to the sound of water running in the bathroom. She looks at the clock. Five-fifteen. What is her mother doing up so early? She pulls her comforter up to her chin and shuts her eyes. Another hour of sleep would be nice. So would the chance to scratch out the entire weekend, all except for dinner with her mom last night, which was actually pretty nice.

Karyn rolls out of bed. She's always been bad at getting back to sleep once she's awake. Maybe she can think of exactly what she'll say to Reed when she sees him in school today. Not that she has any clue what that will be.

The water in the bathroom shuts off. Karyn pulls on her robe and opens her bedroom door, then walks into the hallway. She's almost at the bathroom when the door opens and she collides with the person coming out.

It's not her mom. It's some tall guy wearing boxer shorts and nothing else. Karyn's nose is just inches from his skin.

She chokes on the odor, a disgusting mixture of cigarette smoke and cologne.

Karyn takes a step back. She pulls the belt of her robe tight around her waist. "Who . . . What are you . . . ?"

The man looks uncomfortably toward Ms. Aufiero's bedroom door, as if somehow it might save him from this awkward moment.

Karyn flashes back to when her mom had left last night, on her way to see her *friends* Nora and Meg. She'd warned Karyn that she might be late. Nora was having trouble at work and really needed to talk.

But it had all been a lie, even after the honest moment Karyn had *thought* she and her mother finally reached.

"Who are you?" Karyn asks again.

"I . . . uh . . . I'm Jake. Jake Conroy. A friend of Maggie's."

"You mean my mother!" Karyn says sharply, keeping a steady focus on his forehead. She doesn't want to look down because the guy is practically naked. And she doesn't want to look at his eyes because that would make him real. Real would make her mom a complete hypocrite. A liar.

Ms. Aufiero opens her bedroom door, emerging in a black spaghetti strap nightgown. Both Karyn and Jake turn their heads. She looks right at Karyn, ignoring Jake. "Honey, you're up," she squeaks.

Karyn feels her face flush as the anger builds. "A night with your *girl*friends!" she spits out. "He doesn't look anything like Nora."

Jake shifts from one foot to the other, then turns and slinks back to Karyn's mom's bedroom. Ms. Aufiero touches his shoulder as he passes, and Karyn feels bile rise in her throat.

The hallway suddenly gets smaller. Karyn rubs her eyes. Is this really happening? Maybe she just imagined that guy. Maybe her mom really isn't wearing that awful nightgown and didn't have some guy spend the night in *their house* with Karyn just down the hall.

"Sweetie, please," her mom says. She pauses, glancing between Karyn and her bedroom. Then she quickly moves to shut her bedroom door. She turns back to Karyn, but Karyn starts heading back toward her room.

"Wait," her mom pleads. She follows Karyn, standing in front of her next to Karyn's bedroom door. "I did meet up with Nora and Meg, at that bar on the corner of Spring Street," she explains. "Then I ran into Jake. We'd spoken a few times at the bar before. It's not like he's a stranger." Last night's makeup still lines Ms. Aufiero's eyes.

"A few times before," Karyn says. "Well, I guess that's a good enough reason to bring someone home and sleep with him. It makes sense, you know, with how you were talking last night about taking sex seriously."

Ms. Aufiero cringes. "I know how this looks," she begins. "But you have to understand. This was different. I had just found out that—" She stops, looking at Karyn with a pained expression.

"Found out what?" Karyn demands. "That the guy from Saturday night was busy?"

"No, Karyn, I had just found out that your father is getting remarried!" her mother blurts out, her whole face bright red with anger.

Karyn's jaw drops. She suddenly feels like the air in the hall is charged with energy, like if she tries to take a step, she'll be blocked by the sheer force of the tension surrounding her. She swallows. "Dad's—Dad's getting married?"

Immediately Ms. Aufiero drops her face into her hands. "I never should have let it come out like that," she says through her fingers. "I'm so sorry. I was just so tired of you accusing me, saying those *things* to me." She takes her hands away and looks at Karyn. "Your father sent me an e-mail last night, when I checked the computer right before going out. He wrote that he and Kelly . . . they're getting married." Ms. Aufiero clenches her fists so tightly, Karyn can see the whites of her knuckles. "He wants—wanted—to tell you himself, but he thought I should know first, in case you need help accepting the news." She shakes her head. "Of course he never stopped to wonder if *I'd* have trouble accepting it."

Karyn doesn't know what to think, what to say to her mom, what to feel. It's too much. It's just too much.

"Oh, honey . . . ," her mother says, walking toward her with outstretched arms.

"No, stop," Karyn says, backing up into her bedroom. "Just—I don't want to hear any more."

She shuts the bedroom door and crouches down on the floor, her head pounding. Nothing makes any sense. She's kissed Reed. Lied to T. J. Her mom is sleeping around, and her dad is getting remarried.

Without knowing exactly what she's going to do, Karyn reaches for a pair of sweats on the floor and pulls them on. She takes off her robe and puts on a sweatshirt.

"Please let me in," her mom calls from the other side of the door.

Karyn digs under her bed for her running sneakers and puts them on. The throb in her head is beginning to make her dizzy. She stands up and opens the door.

"What are you doing?" her mother asks.

Get out of my way. She rushes through the hall and down the stairs.

"Honey, please let's talk about this."

What is there to talk about? You're a liar and so am I.

Karyn doesn't grab a jacket. Not even her keys. She pushes through the front door and sprints across the lawn toward the trees bordering the backyard. There's a trail that weaves through miles of woods.

Her legs pick up speed. Cold wind cuts her face. The impact of her feet against the frozen earth hurts, but Karyn doesn't care. She looks down at her legs. Wills them to move faster. It's still dark outside, and Karyn can barely see the branches in her way until it's too late. They scrape her face as she runs. Tears stream from her eyes. She remembers the dream from the other night. It was just like this. She was running through the woods. She didn't know who was chasing her. Now she knows—she wasn't being chased. She was escaping. Escaping her life.

The path is endless, but her legs won't let up. Her lungs burn. A good burn. Something to free her mind. No more thoughts of her mother. Her father. Reed. T. J.

Karyn doesn't know how long she's been running or even where she is when the trail abruptly ends. Suddenly she's standing on a patch of lawn. Somebody's backyard. Her lungs begin to ache. She stops, bends over, rests her hands on her thighs. Her panting slows a bit. Karyn straightens up, looks around. The only sound she can hear is her heartbeat. The sky has gone from dark gray to a soft blue. There are streaks of pink in the distance.

Twenty yards from where she stands is a modest blue colonial with white shutters. The house looks well kept, with fresh paint. A row of bushes line the perimeter of a slate patio. Next to the patio is a set of metal doors leading down to a basement—the only part of the house that doesn't look crisp. The doors are covered with patches of rust.

Karyn stares at the doors. She's been down in that basement. She knows this house. It belongs to Peter Davis.

Except for a light shining through a downstairs window,

the place is dark. *Maybe that's Peter's room.* Karyn walks toward the light. She doesn't know why. Something tells her that window definitely belongs to him.

She passes the metal doors. Doesn't look. Can't bring herself to look. Walks toward the light.

She and Peter have exchanged nothing more than small talk over the past few years. They dated freshman year, briefly, but it was never serious. She can't even remember why it ended. Probably because they were just freshmen and had no idea how to date.

When Karyn is a few feet from the window, she looks around, suddenly self-conscious. *What am I doing? And what time is it?*

She takes another step, then cranes her neck to peer inside. Peter sits in his wheelchair at his desk, concentrating hard on a textbook lying open on his lap.

Why would he be studying at this hour? The Peter I knew never cracked a book.

Light comes from a desk lamp. It bathes his body in a soft, soothing warmth.

She lifts her fingers to the glass. It's crazy, but she can't stop herself. She taps on the window.

• • •

"So, you make a habit of spying on people first thing in the morning?" Peter asks as he shuts the window that Karyn Aufiero just climbed through.

Karyn responds with a nervous laugh.

Maybe you could clue me in on why you're here?

Karyn doesn't say anything. She just stands there, staring around the room with a confused look on her face, like she was just magically beamed here instead of having obviously shown up of her own free will.

Finally her eyes land on the textbook on Peter's desk. "I'm sorry—you're busy," she says, pulling the sleeves of her sweatshirt over her hands.

"Oh no, don't worry about it. I went to this new physical therapy session yesterday and my arm muscles are killing me. I couldn't sleep, so I figured I'd catch up on some reading."

"Wow, physical therapy, that's great," Karyn says.

Yeah, really great, but why are you here?

Karyn's teeth begin to chatter. "I guess you're wondering what I'm doing here."

Peter wheels over to his bed and tosses her an extra blanket. "Kinda."

"Thanks," she says as she wraps the blanket around her body. She sits in the chair by his window.

Okay, this is weird. The last time they really talked was during their pathetic month-long relationship freshman year. It hadn't taken her long to decide that she was way too cool for him. Peter was just some geeky freshman, while Karyn was on her way to becoming, well, Karyn Aufiero.

Karyn sucks in a deep breath. "Honestly, I don't even know how I got—I mean, I just started running, and I kept going, and then I was . . . here."

Peter nods, even though he has no clue what she's talking about.

"It's just I—I had this fight with my mom last night," she begins, the words coming out on top of each other. "She found—well, she went through my stuff and found a box of condoms."

Peter's eyebrows shoot up. Did she actually just tell him that?

"Then I get the whole sex lecture, which is absurd coming from her because my mom has a new date, like, every night. And she tells me how to behave? I'm not even having sex! Which is another story," she says, throwing her weight back into the chair.

Peter doesn't say anything. He can tell she's not finished. Even if she was finished, he's not sure he'd have a response.

Karyn sighs. "You don't want to hear this, do you? God, I'm rambling." She rubs her temples, then glances around the room again. "I swear, I really don't know why I'm here," she says, sounding as puzzled as he feels. "It's just suddenly there I was, standing outside your house. I saw you reading, and I . . . I don't know."

Peter is still shocked that Karyn is sitting in his bedroom. No makeup. No cool clothes. Not surrounded by the in crowd. Talking about some fight with her mom and condoms she's not using. Whatever's up with her, it must be pretty bad if she ran all the way over here and had the nerve to knock on his window.

"So anyway," Karyn says, "my mom and I finally had this whole mother-daughter bonding session after the fight was over. Everything was cool. Then I wake up this morning and find a strange guy wearing boxers in the hall. And *then* my mom comes out in this cheesy nightgown."

Peter remembers how upset Karyn used to get when she overheard her parents fighting, back when he was dating her. He could tell even then that things weren't going in a good direction for her family.

"Sounds like a bad way to start the day," Peter offers, knowing it sounds lame. But what the hell is he supposed to say? Is she looking for advice or a place to vent? Insight doesn't come to him right off the bat. Especially for someone he barely knows anymore.

Karyn spaces out on a spot on his floor, and Peter looks at the history book lying open on his desk. No chance he'll get to finish reading before school. *She seems pretty upset. But I still don't get why she's coming to me with this. Why not one of her friends? Why not her boyfriend, T. J. Frasier? Why not Reed? Everyone knows those two are joined at the hip.*

Peter looks out the window at the trail that edges his property. As a kid, he played this Indiana Jones game where he'd explore the woods. Climbing trees, crossing streams, building huts with branches, even killing worms, which he would pretend to eat. Each time he was in search of something different. He never knew what it was until he found it. Maybe an oddly shaped rock, a cluster of moss, or a cracked bottle buried in the dirt. Now he can't even wheel himself along the path. Too many rocks and branches. But Karyn can run through the woods and not even notice. She can be so wrapped up in her own life that she's oblivious to the simple fact that she's got legs to take her away from her problems. Does she ever even think about Meena Miller, someone who used to be one of her friends? Does she have any clue what Meena's been going through? Yeah, parent stuff sucks, but come on—there are people who have it much worse.

Karyn stands up and folds the blanket. "I should go," she says. "I shouldn't be here, complaining about this to you."

"Yeah, maybe not," Peter can't help saying. Karyn looks at him in surprise. "Well, we've barely spoken since you ditched me freshman year," he adds. "And you know, I'm sorry you're fighting with your mom, but if you opened your eyes, you could see that some of us are dealing with a lot more."

The minute he says it, he wishes he could take it back. He's always saying how much he hates being pitied. Now he's asking her to do just that.

Karyn's face scrunches up in obvious embarrassment. "Oh my gosh, Peter . . . I'm sorry. You're right."

Peter shakes his head. "No, I didn't mean that," he snaps, angry at himself, not her. He inhales deeply, then meets her gaze. "I know how close you and your mom used to be, and it must be really hard to feel like you can't talk to her anymore."

Karyn bites her lip, nodding back at him.

"And I think it's kind of cool that you ended up here, actually." He pauses, then starts to smile. "I mean, whose shoulder does one of the most popular girls at Falls High want to cry on? That's right, look no further, ladies and gentlemen—it's the one and only Peter Davis, former king of the outcasts."

"Come on, you weren't an outcast," she protests.

Peter narrows his eyes at her and she holds his gaze a second, then they both start to laugh.

"Okay, fine," she says. "But that's definitely not how *I* see you." She tilts her head to the side. "Seriously, Peter—thanks."

He grins. "No problem. My door—uh, window—is always open."

• • •

Later that morning, Peter lingers just inside the school entrance, waiting for Meena. He yawns and tilts his head from side to side. That surprise visit from Karyn gave him a temporary rush of energy, but after going through the morning routine and coming to school, he's starting to feel the effects of getting so little sleep last night.

When he first heard the tap at his window earlier, he'd actually thought it could be Meena. She never returned his call last night, and he can't stop worrying about her.

You don't even know what Clayton did to her. Maybe the problem really can be solved now that he's moving out. She seemed pretty convinced of that.

Peter watches the doors swing open and shut. No Meena.

Who are you kidding? She's a basket case. That girl needs help. If she would let me in, maybe I could . . . man, what could I even do? I just need to figure out what's going on.

Peter rolls himself off to the side, where he can avoid the regular stampede of students hurrying to homeroom. He also wants to avoid his former friends Max Kang, Keith Kleiner, and Doug Anderson. If they're together—which they always are—Peter's sure they're going to give him a hard time. "Hey, geek, heard there's an opening on the debate team." "If you join the science club, mind swipin' us some drugs?" *Losers. I wonder what convenience store they ripped off this weekend? Or what girls they managed to harass on Saturday night?*

"Hey, Peter, here you are."

He turns and sees Jane Scott standing beside him, loaded down with her stuffed backpack on one arm and her sax case in the other hand. "Hey, Jane. Good weekend?"

She shrugs. "Weekend? What's that?"

Peter laughs. He's surprised that she hasn't already positioned herself behind his chair, ready to wheel him to homeroom in record time. He really should buy a stopwatch.

"Ready?" she asks.

"I'm gonna wait for Meena," he answers. "I need to ask her a question. She can take me to homeroom."

"Wow. The one morning I've got time to kill and you don't need my help," Jane says.

Peter looks at his watch. "Has the great Jane Scott *ever* had eleven minutes to kill?"

Jane frowns, and Peter braces himself to get snapped at—something he's gotten used to with Jane, even if he hasn't quite gotten down the skill of predicting which comments will provoke her.

But all she says is, "Well, if she doesn't show, you're on your own."

"I'll be fine," he says.

She shrugs. "Okay. See you later, then."

Jane walks off and Peter continues scanning the crowd for Meena. There's the goth girl whose mom is friends with his mom. The kid who gets a new tattoo every other month. Jeremy Mandile and Reed Frasier hidden beneath their baseball caps.

Peter checks the time. Eight minutes until homeroom. When he looks up again, he sees Meena, entering through the far door. *Finally.*

"Meena," he yells, then navigates his wheelchair through the crowd.

She turns around. Her hair is pulled off her face in a loose ponytail. But her outfit, as on most days, consists of baggy black corduroys and a gray sweater that looks like it came from one of her brothers' hand-me-down piles.

"Hey," she says.

"Did you get my message last night?" he asks, studying her expression closely. No real change there.

"Yeah. But I crashed early, so it wasn't until this morning." She brings a hand to her mouth and lets out a grating smoker's cough. He actually hasn't seen her smoking lately, but maybe she's still doing it when she's alone.

Peter exhales. "So everything is okay, then?" *Would you relax? She's gonna start avoiding you if you don't take it easy.*

Meena looks around them nervously, even though no one's casting them a second glance. "Yeah, Peter. Everything's okay. Can we—can you just drop the whole thing?"

Peter wheels closer to her, keeping his voice down. "Meena, how am I supposed to drop it after how upset you were that night at your house?"

Meena shifts her gaze to the floor.

"Listen," he says, trying to sound gentle. "I don't know what happened. I don't *need* to know what happened. But someone does. Please tell someone, Meena. It's not going to be okay until you do."

Nothing.

Maybe I should switch gears here, give her a little time.

"Okay, maybe you're right—maybe I need to lighten up," he says, wondering if it sounds as absurd to her as it does to him, under the circumstances. But at this point he'll try anything. "How about we get together after school and talk about something else? Maybe we could do something . . . fun?"

"I'm baby-sitting for Trace while Steven and Lydia meet with their realtor," she says, kicking at the floor.

"Too bad. I was gonna suggest taking a step up from the diner and going for coffee at Geoffrey's."

"That does sound cool," she says with a tiny smile. A smile from Meena, no matter how small, is like gold. "Can we do it another time?"

"Anytime," he replies.

She nods, then seems to remember something. "How about tomorrow?" she blurts out.

"Yeah, okay," he says. "Any particular reason?" he can't help adding. It's obvious there is one.

"I've got another stupid psychiatrist appointment tomorrow, with Dr. Lansky," Meena replies. She starts shredding the corner of her notebook. "I was wondering if maybe . . . you'd come with me."

"Sure," Peter says, trying not to show how surprised he is that she asked. "But am I allowed?"

"Well, you couldn't come in with me or anything. But you could wait outside. I mean it would be cool if after we could hang out, go get that coffee at Geoffrey's. But only if you're free because it's no big deal, really. . . ."

"I'll be there," he says, feeling a smile come to his lips. Meena's starting to trust him. He didn't even know how important that is to him, but suddenly it means everything.

• • •

Karyn studies the steaming vat of kielbasa in front of her. Mondays are International Day in the Falls High cafeteria, and every week the dish they serve is a little scarier.

Karyn shrinks away from the sour smell and walks over to where Gemma Masters and Jeannie Chang are waiting in the sandwich line, babbling about their weekends.

Karyn tunes them out and examines the deli sandwiches lined up under a glass window. Wilting lettuce, dry bread, and meager amounts of cold cuts. She looks around the cafeteria for better options. She hasn't eaten anything all day and she's pretty hungry. More hungry than usual since she went running this morning.

That was a pretty crazy experience. She hasn't seen Peter Davis in the halls yet today. She's not sure if she wants to run into him or not. Somehow when she was at his house, alone with him, she felt safe in a way she hadn't felt all weekend as her whole life spun out of control. But she's not sure if she'd feel the same way with Peter here in school or if she'd just be embarrassed for freaking out on him this morning.

Pretty ironic—me feeling safe at Peter Davis's house. There was a time when she didn't think she'd ever be able to step foot inside there again. Even when they dated, she never went into his house.

Karyn sighs, feeling utterly exhausted. The cafeteria's bright lights aren't helping, and neither are the heavy smells of lunch food and the dozens of bodies knocking into her. She should have skipped school, like she'd thought about on the way home from Peter's. But it had just seemed like too much trouble, with her mom being the school guidance counselor. She can't handle another mother-daughter confrontation just yet.

Karyn turns from the sandwich counter and wanders over to the salad bar. More wilting lettuce.

"Hey, Karyn."

She looks up and sees Jeremy Mandile. Automatically her eyes move to the space next to him, and her breath catches.

Reed.

Suddenly she's slammed with a whirl of feelings—everything from excitement to fear to pain so intense, she almost doubles over. It's like she's reliving what happened between them yesterday, but her memory's on warp speed, so it's all jumbled together. She feels the electricity that coursed through her as her hands touched his skin, the sheer thrill of that mind-blowing kiss, the gentle sensation of his hand on her lower back. At the same time she's as scared as she was when he pulled back and looked at her with so much horror in his eyes. And the pain of his rejection—of the cold, harsh words he threw at her—it's as raw as if he just said those things a second ago, here in this cafeteria.

She takes a deep breath. Looks at his face. It's totally blank. Not a single clue as to what he's thinking.

You have to calm down, get yourself under control. Another deep breath. *Say hi. Act normal.*

Karyn forces a smile. "What's up?"

"Not much," Jeremy answers. "What looks good today?"

"See for yourself," Karyn says, gesturing toward the

kielbasa. She looks at Reed, but he's staring in a different direction. Avoiding meeting her gaze.

Act normal.

"Hi, Reed," she practically shouts. *Normal, not demented.*

Reed gives a slight nod, still not looking at her.

Oh God, she's not going to cry right here in front of everyone, is she?

She shoots Jeremy a tight smile, like everything's fine. Nice try. There's no way he's gonna miss that something is off between her and Reed.

"Well, from the look on your face, I guess the food's pretty bad today," Jeremy says, clearly trying to fill the awkwardness somehow.

"Uh . . . yeah . . . it's brutal," Karyn says, blinking like crazy. Reed wanders over to the sandwich line. How is this possible? How could her best friend in the world act like she's a stranger?

"I'm one of the few fans of International Day," Jeremy says, rubbing his stomach.

"Go for it," Karyn says, her voice barely above a whisper.

As soon as Reed's out of earshot, Jeremy drops the fake smile and leans in closer to her. "Hey, what's up with you guys?" he asks.

So Reed didn't tell him. She'd been wondering . . . they do live together now, after all. But who is she kidding? That kiss—the one that had changed everything for her—it didn't mean a thing to Reed. He and Jeremy had probably spent last night talking about important stuff in their lives, like football.

"Just a stupid fight," Karyn mutters, looking over at the back of Reed's head. "I'm gonna hit the salad bar," she says.

"We've got a table. Come sit with us," Jeremy urges.

Karyn just shakes her head and steps into line for the salad bar, heaping lettuce onto her plate. *I don't get it.* She knows there are guys like that out there, but not Reed. He's never been one of those jerks who are corrupted purely by the presence of a Y chromosome. She moves from lettuce to cucumbers. *So what, then?* What about that kiss had made him shut down?

T. J. The same reason she'd reeled from the whole experience. She knows Reed's horrified by what they did to his brother. She's just as horrified. But at the same time—as crazy as it sounds—it feels like that kiss had nothing to do with T. J., like it happened in a space outside the normal world where she and T. J. are dating. But that *is* crazy. Right now everything's crazy.

All she knows is that she can't take Reed ignoring her—it's almost worse than having him yell at her. No, it *is* worse. Because it's like suddenly, she's nothing to him. The way it was with her parents after their divorce—one day, her mom was her dad's wife. The next, she was Karyn's mother, but that was it. There wasn't even any fighting anymore because he just didn't *care.* He had a new girlfriend, a new home. *A new girlfriend who's about to be a new wife,* Karyn remembers, her head starting to pound.

98

She remembers not being able to comprehend how that could happen to her parents, how her mom could just cease to matter to her dad. Now Karyn can begin to imagine what it must have felt like for her mom, and she wonders how she ever survived it. Yeah, Reed's a friend, not a boyfriend. But he's her *best* friend, and for him to just abandon her like this . . . she's so hurt, so angry, she doesn't even know what to do with it all.

"Some cucumbers with your salad?"

Karyn looks up and sees Tim Cavanaugh, the school's number-one swimmer, standing opposite her at the salad bar.

Karyn looks down at her plate. It's loaded with cucumber slices. "Guess I spaced out," she says, putting some back.

"Better to space out on cucumbers than that nasty-looking coleslaw," Tim says, pointing to a bucket swimming with mayonnaise. He gives her a big smile, and she remembers hearing that Tim used to have a crush on her. She wonders if he still does.

"Definitely," she says, reaching for the carrots. On impulse she looks over her right shoulder and catches Reed watching her and Tim.

She turns her attention back to Tim. Karyn's always thought he's cute, but he's not really her type. He's tall and lanky, with shaggy blond hair that hangs down almost to his shoulders. A little too much of the hippie look for her. But maybe . . . well, maybe there's a way to play this.

Karyn leans over the salad bar and picks up a cherry tomato with her fingers. "So do you *ever* think they'll let cheerleaders cheer at swim meets?" she asks. "I'm so sick of football."

Tim's grin widens. "I think they're afraid you guys would slip and fall in," he jokes. "Although I'm sure most guys would love a soaking wet cheerleader."

Karyn pops the tomato in her mouth. Out of the corner of her eye, she sees Reed's baseball hat. He's still facing her direction. *Good.* She pushes a strand of hair behind her ear. "What good's a swim meet without school spirit?" she says coyly.

"You're right," Tim agrees. "Maybe I can convince Coach that poolside would be a lot more entertaining with you guys around."

"I'm sure you won't have any problem. You're basically the entire swim team," she says, squeezing his elbow. At this point, there's no need to check if Reed's watching. His eyes are burning holes through her back.

Tim blushes. "Do me a favor and don't say that to the rest of the team."

Karyn throws him a flirty smile, complete with some classic eye twinkle. "I'm gonna go pay," she says. "I'll see you around." She picks up her tray and turns toward the cash register.

There. Now Reed will see that just because he can act like she doesn't exist, it doesn't mean another guy wouldn't jump at the chance to talk to her. Karyn pays for her salad, then walks out into the seating area, scanning the room for Gemma and Amy.

"What was that all about?"

Karyn spins around and sees Reed's face just inches from her own, but barely recognizes his angry expression.

"Oh, so you're talking to me now?" she demands.

Reed scoffs, then pulls her aside to a quiet corner by the wall. "Karyn, what is the matter with you?"

Karyn takes a step back. His voice holds the same bitterness it did yesterday. "Nothing's the matter with me," she says quietly. This wasn't the reaction she expected.

"Then what was that little thing with Tim Cavanaugh about?"

Karyn shrugs. "We were just talking. What's the—"

"Just talking?" Reed shakes his head in disgust. "Didn't look that way to me."

"Since when is it your business who I talk to, anyway?" she asks.

For a second Karyn can see her friend again—the sweet, vulnerable Reed she's known forever staring at her like he's as hurt as she is. Then his eyes darken, and the anger returns to his features. "What about T. J.?" he asks in a low, hard voice. "Isn't it his business?"

Karyn glances away, guilt washing over her. First she cheats on T. J. with another guy. Then she flirts with someone just to get that other guy's attention. *But this has nothing to do with*

T. J., she reminds herself. She doesn't know how or why. But somehow it just doesn't.

"I—I would never hurt T. J.," she begins. And she really does mean it, as insane as it must sound.

Reed's eyes widen. "Oh, really? Then what the hell do you think you were doing yesterday?" He pauses, glancing around to make sure no one can hear him. "How exactly was kissing *me* not hurting my brother?" he finishes.

Karyn takes in a sharp breath. *But I didn't,* she thinks. *I didn't kiss you to hurt anyone. I kissed you because . . . because it felt like the only thing I could do.* "Is that all you care about?" she blurts out, near tears. "Your brother?"

Reed just looks at her, then shakes his head again slowly. "The thing is, I thought you cared about him, too," he says. And then he walks away.

CHAPTER SiX

Jane pushes her way through the side door of the cafeteria and into the sunny courtyard. She blinks at the bright light—she's not used to being outside in the middle of the day. Not used to spending any part of the daylight hours without her nose in a book. It's nice out, maybe even in the fifties. Warm for November in Winetka Falls.

She checks her watch, then scans the courtyard for Peter. Only five minutes until lunch period is over. Out of habit, Jane begins to make a mental list of the things she's supposed to do today. Then she stops herself, remembering that there's no longer anything she has to do since she's ruined her chances for a future, anyway.

Jane walks to an empty picnic table directly in the sunlight. She sits down and lets the sun warm her skin.

"Jane, I don't think I've ever seen you out here during lunch. Giving yourself a break?"

Jane looks over and sees Mrs. Gormley, her homeroom teacher, sitting at another table with two other teachers. *Giving myself a break? Is that what I'm doing?*

"Yeah, too nice to be inside," she replies.

"Good. It's about time you let yourself off the hook."

Jane nods awkwardly. She's not sure what to do with herself. A group of guys toss a Frisbee around a few yards away. Everyone else is lounging around talking, laughing, eating, or just scoping out the scene.

Jane watches the activity unfold around her like she's somewhere else, not sitting right in the middle of it. The sun feels good. Healthy. How is it that she has missed even the simplest of pleasures for the greater part of her academic life? Sunlight. Laughter. Friends.

She notices Sarah Styrons walk by with Jonah Berg. They're holding hands. Jane knows Sarah from the film reviews she writes for the Web site. Jonah's always in a school play. They're both smart, and they do a fair number of activities. *When did they get together? I can't imagine watching TV for twenty minutes, much less having time to find a boyfriend.*

She's barely even noticed the guys at Falls High. Well, except for one guy . . . but that was so long ago. Her freshman year, she'd been practically obsessed with senior Quinn Saunders, captain of the Academic Decathlon and editor of the Web site. But that had been different. Quinn was as driven as she was, involved in just as many activities and equally devoted to getting top grades. She'd known she didn't have a chance with him, so her feelings for him were more admiration. He was a role model for what she hoped to be. And every time he gave her the slightest compliment, she'd run the words over and over in her head before going to sleep that night. Respect from someone like Quinn was major.

Quinn never talked down to me, even though I was younger. He seemed to think I was going somewhere with my life, just like he was. God, what would Quinn Saunders think if he saw her now?

The door to the cafeteria opens and she sees Meena Miller helping Peter over the bump in the doorway. They say something to each other, and then Meena goes back inside. Jane waves to Peter and he wheels in her direction.

"Quick question before class," he says as he approaches. "Was the assignment to finish the book or just get to chapter eighteen? Please say chapter eighteen."

Jane shrugs.

"What, you're not gonna tell me?" Peter says. "Come on, you've got to give me a break here."

Jane smiles, feeling a strange sense of anticipation. "I didn't do the reading," she says. "Didn't even look at the syllabus. Can't help you."

Peter gapes. "You're kidding. What will Harvard say?"

"Oh, please," she says, enjoying his reaction even though inside, it still hurts like crazy at the same time. *When was the last time I did something that surprised someone?*

"I can't believe it," he says, slouching back in his chair.

"What can't you believe? It's not like I'm perfect."

"Okay, so maybe you're not perfect," Peter says, "but you're not exactly a slacker, either." He stops, gives her a grin. "You know, Jane, being a true slacker takes hard work. Slacker qualities don't grow on trees."

It takes her a second to realize he's throwing her own words back at her, from the time she freaked out on him in the cafeteria. She knows she should be annoyed, but instead she just laughs.

"Very cute," she says. "Okay, time for class." She walks around behind his chair and starts to wheel him inside, but they only make it a few feet down the hall when she spots Sumit heading right toward them.

"Hey, Jane, have you forgotten our bet?" he asks.

She gives him a tight smile. *Okay, I told Reed about my scores. Now I have to tell Sumit.*

"So come on," he says, his dark eyes gleaming with curiosity. "Have your scores finally come?"

Tell him the truth.

"Actually," she starts, steeling herself for the big confession. And then she realizes—she can't do it. Telling Reed was one thing. But Sumit has been her biggest competitor for so long . . . she just can't admit to having messed things up so badly. "I . . . uh . . . I called about the scores yesterday. There was some machine problem or something, so they're delayed."

"Oh," Sumit says, his face falling. "That sucks. I

hope it doesn't mess with your college applications."

"Yeah," Jane says blandly.

"I'm gonna be late. You've got to tell me when you find out," Sumit says, taking off down the hall.

Peter, who's stayed quiet during the whole conversation, turns to look up at her, an obvious question in his eyes. He knows something's wrong. But whatever he sees on her face causes him to turn back around.

"Thanks," she says quietly. He just nods, and she resumes wheeling him toward class.

• • •

". . . ten, eleven, twelve."

Reed groans and drops a pair of thirty-pound dumbbells on the floor of the gym weight room. He shakes out his arms. Five sets done. He can handle a couple more. Keeping his mind occupied is key.

More precisely, keeping his mind off Karyn is key.

But that's starting to seem completely impossible. Because no matter where he tries to take his mind, it just comes back to Karyn. How it felt to kiss her. How *T. J.* would feel if he knew Reed kissed her. And he can't stop wondering how the Karyn he thought he knew inside and out could actually act the way she did today in the cafeteria. How she could have kissed him in the first place, when she's dating his brother.

Reed reaches for the dumbbells and grunts as he starts in on another set of arm curls.

107

One . . . not possible, never gonna happen.

Two . . . I'm T. J.'s little . . . three . . . brother.

Four . . . little! God, I hate that.

Five . . . her lips were . . . six . . .

So soft . . . seven . . . so . . .

Eight . . . so wrong.

He lets out a groan and drops the weights to the floor.

"Haven't you ever heard of burnout?"

Reed turns to Jeremy, who's doing ab crunches on the floor. They've been working out together for years.

"I'm fine," Reed mutters.

"You'd better take it easy." Jeremy tosses him a towel.

Reed wipes away his sweat. He pulls his wet maroon T-shirt away from his body. Taking it easy is the last thing he wants to do. His adrenaline has been revved ever since he blew up at Karyn in the cafeteria. She was out of line, yeah, but he really lost it. Just like he did yesterday, at her place. It was just that seeing her flirt with Cavanaugh like that had made him insanely jealous. And all that did was get him more pissed, at himself, at Karyn. Because what right does *he* have to be jealous? It's like every second he's finding a new way to betray his brother, no matter how hard he tries not to.

Reed gets up and walks over to the bench press. Jeremy isn't stupid. He knows something's up. But there's no way Reed can admit what a slimy thing he did, kissing his own brother's girlfriend. And liking it. *Loving it.*

Reed sets up the bench press with more weights than

usual. He might as well take advantage of this supercharge he's on and build up his muscles. He lies down and raises his arms to the cold metal bar. His muscles tense as he exerts every ounce of leftover energy. The bar won't budge.

Come on, Reed.

Not an inch.

He tries harder. *Just . . . just . . . lift the damn thing.*

No use. He lets go of the bar and his arms flap to his sides. His entire body tingles, a buzz that he can practically hear inside his own head. Reed sits up and shakes out his muscles. The feeling is disturbingly familiar. Sort of like how he felt when Karyn kissed him.

"Damn," he says out loud.

Jeremy looks his way. "What's up?"

"Nothing," Reed says. He swings his legs over the side of the bench. How could he have done this to his brother? Not just the kiss. How could he have let himself have feelings for T. J.'s girlfriend? After everything T. J. has done for him.

"Okay, buddy," Jeremy says, "enough with the athletically challenged bit over here. What's up?"

Don't start, man. Leave me alone.

"Not that you really have to tell me," Jeremy says. "I know it's Karyn."

Reed looks at Jeremy. "How's Emily?" he asks.

Jeremy takes a long swig from his water bottle. "She's fine. Just keeps asking when I'm coming home."

Reed and Jeremy stare at the row of free weights.

"Look, I get that you don't want to talk about Karyn," Jeremy says. "But if you change your mind . . ."

"Whatever," Reed replies, throwing himself back so he's reclining on the weight bench. *I can keep telling myself to get over her, but what's the use? She kissed me and I wanted it. There's nobody else who makes me feel like she does. I'm just going to have to get used to that feeling. And not act on it.*

"We're pathetic," Jeremy says, snapping his towel at Reed's leg.

"Hey," Reed yells, sitting up. He rubs his calf. "That actually hurt. What are you trying to do—paralyze me so that I can't run away when you start in about Karyn?"

"Actually, it would take more than a towel to paralyze someone," a voice says from across the room.

Jeremy and Reed both whip their heads around, and Reed sees Peter Davis sitting in his wheelchair in the corner, holding two dumbbells. They hadn't even noticed him come in. Reed wonders how long Peter's been here.

"Man, I'm—uh . . . really sorry," Reed stammers. "I didn't see . . . I mean if I had known . . ."

"Relax, Frasier," Peter says, smiling. "I just thought I'd put your mind at ease."

Reed's throat tightens. He looks nervously at Jeremy, whose face is beet red.

"Really, guys, I was just kidding around," Peter adds.

Say something, Reed thinks, giving Jeremy a look. But Jeremy is just as embarrassed as Reed.

110

"Listen, if you guys don't loosen up," Peter says, "I'm gonna kick your asses. I'll be out of the chair in no time; it's no big deal."

"That's great," Jeremy says. "Did they tell you that?"

Peter's smile fades a fraction. "Not exactly," he says. "But it's definitely happening. And in the meantime, I'm working my upper body to keep up my strength. I have to say, though, I'm pretty impressed with you jocks. This weight-lifting thing isn't easy."

"It helps to have someone spot you," Reed says. "Jeremy and I come together a lot." He looks over at Jeremy, then has an idea. "Hey, you know, if you ever need someone to work out with, I'm here, like, every day."

"Yeah, maybe," Peter says with a shrug.

Reed isn't even sure why he said it. He hasn't hung around Peter since . . . well, since pretty much right after the single worst day of his life. And that was a long time ago.

"Just let me know. We jocks love lifting," Reed jokes.

"Thanks, man," Peter replies.

Reed and Jeremy return to their exercises and Peter wheels himself back over to the free weights.

Reed watches out of the corner of his eye as Peter struggles to keep going, obviously winded. What an amazing turnaround. Before his accident, the guy had a permanent I-hate-the-world scowl on his face. But now he just seems . . . different. Like he's got things under control in a way Reed would give anything for right about now.

Maybe that's why he made the offer. Maybe Reed's hoping that if he spends more time around Peter, some of that ability to take it all in stride will rub off on him.

• • •

It's Monday evening and Karyn's sitting with Jeremy in a corner booth at the Falls Diner, pushing around a pile of french fries with her fork. She'd been happy to accept Jeremy's invitation to come get dinner here, since she's in no hurry to face her mom. But now she's wishing she and Jeremy had chosen somewhere else to go. Large, noisy, annoying families surround them.

She was outside the locker room after cheerleading practice when she saw Jeremy at the other end of the hall. He was on his way back to the Frasiers' house. Reed had bolted after football practice for a shift at TCBY, and Jeremy didn't feel like spending the evening alone with Mrs. Frasier. At the time, Karyn was starving. After the disaster with Reed in the cafeteria earlier today, she'd spent the rest of her lunch period poking at her salad.

But once she got here, her appetite disappeared. Maybe because sitting across the table from Reed's best friend makes it pretty impossible not to think about Reed.

"I'm just not hungry," she complains, watching Jeremy twirl spaghetti around his fork.

"So why did you order the burger deluxe?" Jeremy asks.

"Bad choice." At first, she had thought a thick, greasy burger might distract her from the anarchy going on in her brain. Now all she can manage is a few sips of water.

"Okay, I thought maybe you'd tell me on your own, but it doesn't really look like it," Jeremy says. He leans forward. "What's wrong?"

"Nothing," Karyn says.

"Then why have you told me three times that Amy Santisi sprained her ankle during practice? And why have you only taken two pathetic bites of your food?"

Karyn puts down her fork. "I don't know. Guess I'm just distracted."

"I know it's about Reed," Jeremy says. "There was a serious cold war going on between you two in the cafeteria today. I've never seen you guys like that before."

Karyn draws in a shaky breath, recalling Reed's face when he yelled at her this afternoon. *The way he looked at me. Like he hates me. Like he thinks I'm disgusting. As disgusting as—oh God, as disgusting as my mother.*

She stares hard at her plate, willing herself not to cry.

"Look," Jeremy continues when she doesn't respond. "You guys have feelings for each other, right?"

Karyn jerks her gaze up to his. "What?"

"Karyn, I'm sorry, but it's pretty obvious to anyone who cares about either of you."

Karyn feels her face start to redden. Anyone who cares about her or Reed . . . "T. J.?" she blurts out. "You think T. J.—"

"No, Karyn, I don't think he has a clue," Jeremy says quickly. "I'm sorry, I shouldn't have said it like that. It's just

113

obvious to *me* because you guys are my best friends."

Karyn picks up her fork again, starts moving the french fries around her plate.

"So, did you have a fight about something?"

She hesitates, then nods, even though the word *fight* doesn't seem to fit. But what does?

"Well, I don't know what it was about, but I can guess," he says.

She doesn't say anything.

"I think I've learned some major lessons about this kind of stuff recently," Jeremy says. "About how wrong it is to be with someone you don't really love, at least not in that way. And how much it sucks to blow it with someone who could make you really happy." He sighs. "I was such a jerk to Josh after he kissed me at that party, when everything came out at school. . . . I still don't know if I wrecked any chance I may have had with him."

Karyn looks at Jeremy, tilting her head in sympathy. "I'm sorry, Jeremy, I haven't even asked about things with Josh. Have you talked to him at all lately?"

He gives his head a quick shake. "No. But don't worry about it—we're talking about you and Reed here. And how you feel about him."

Karyn picks apart her burger. She wasn't expecting this. It's hard enough to admit to herself that she has feelings for Reed, but to someone else—that means the feelings are real.

"My point is, it's time for you guys to be honest about

114

this. Karyn, I know Reed—he is so crazy about you."

Karyn feels a twinge of hope. "He—he told you that?" she asks, knowing she sounds pathetic and not even caring anymore.

Jeremy frowns, and Karyn sinks down into the booth.

"No, he didn't tell me—but there's no way he would. Not while you're going out with T. J. But I swear, I'm right about this. Every time you walk into a room, he looks at you like no one else even exists. You guys have your own jokes, your own rituals, and you basically spend all your free time together."

Norma comes by and fills their water glasses. Karyn takes a long sip. The water cools the burning sensation in her throat.

Maybe I wasn't imagining the way Reed looked at me yesterday. Maybe he does care. But if he does, then why is he being so horrible to me?

One way or another, she has to find out the truth. Right now she's so confused, she has no idea what she really wants. But she does know that Jeremy's right—she can't spend her life with the wrong person. She's seen what happened to her mom, and there's no way she'll let herself end up with someone who seems perfect but isn't going to make her happy.

CHAPTER SEVEN

A light rain drums on the hood of Karyn's car Tuesday morning. She's waiting in the school parking lot, watching students hurry toward the front entrance. The weather really hasn't helped her mood. Neither did her mother's let's-pretend-nothing-happened attitude this morning. She'd actually made Karyn breakfast, something that never happens on a school day. Fresh fruit, eggs, and juice.

Karyn had blurted something out about needing to get to school early for a meeting and rushed out the door. Luckily, even though she and her mom come to the same place every day, they don't usually drive together since Karyn has to stay later for cheerleading practice.

Now that she's here, she's in no hurry to get inside. She's mesmerized by the raindrops hitting her windshield, rolling down the glass. They just keep coming.

Why does everything in her life feel like it's either-or? It started with her parents. They split up, and there was no more one family, one house. She was either with her mom or with her dad. One or the other. Now there's Reed and T. J. She's on the edge of losing her best friend or her boyfriend, or maybe both. What if she had the choice to salvage just one relationship? Which would it be?

Karyn's cell phone rings. She digs through her bag.

"Hello?"

"Hey, babe. It's me," T. J.'s gruff morning voice says.

Karyn's grip on the phone tightens. "Hey, you," she says. *Relax, it's not like he can read your mind.* "What are you doing up so early?"

"I wanted to catch you before school started. To check in about the weekend. Did you find out if you can come up?" he asks. His voice is as hopeful and heartbreaking as the look on a puppy's face when it doesn't want you to walk out the door.

Karyn hasn't even thought about this weekend at all.

"Karyn?"

"Yeah, I, um, I haven't gotten to . . ." She trails off as she sees Reed's familiar blue Subaru pull into a spot a few spaces away. She can vaguely make out his profile.

Karyn's heart begins to pound.

"Karyn, is something wrong?" T. J. asks.

Would you get a grip? "No, no. I'm just still finishing up some homework." She watches through her side mirror as Reed gets out of his car. "Um, Teej, there's just a lot going on with my family right now. I'm not sure what's up for the weekend. But I'll let you know soon. I promise."

T. J. lets out a disappointed sigh. "Okay, well—just let me know. I love you," he says warmly.

Say it back. Say you miss him. You can't wait to see him.

Karyn opens her mouth to speak, but then Reed hurries past her car. His jacket is pulled over his head to shield himself from the rain.

"I promise I'll let you know soon," she says.

"Try and make it really soon."

The rain drums steadily on the roof of the car while Karyn searches for something to say.

"Karyn?"

"Yeah?"

"Did I tell you I loved you?"

Karyn shuts her eyes. Her heart suddenly weighs double. "Yeah, Teej, you told me. I . . . I love you, too." The words sound clumsy. She's no longer sure what they mean anymore. But she wouldn't have said them if she didn't mean them, right? Even if things are complicated, she still knows that she cares about T. J.

"Good. I'll talk to you soon. Bye."

Karyn hits the off button on her phone and tosses it into her bag. She steps out of her car, shivering. All trace of yesterday's gorgeous weather is gone. Karyn walks across the parking lot, hugging her arms around her body.

Danny Chaiken and Cori Lerner are huddled together to the right of the entrance, laughing about something. She nods a quick hello as she passes them. *They look so happy.*

The rain doesn't bother happy people. God, I totally forget what that feels like.

Karyn pulls at the heavy door, anxious to catch up to Reed. But as soon as she's inside, she stops. Reed's standing right there, talking to Shaheem Dobi. The front of his dark blue shirt is splattered with rain, and his cheeks are flushed from the cold. And he's smiling. Smiling at Shaheem like his life is absolutely fine, like there's no reason not to smile.

Has she smiled once in the past couple of days?

"Hey, Karyn," Shaheem says, catching sight of her.

"Hey," she says, feeling completely out of place in her own school lobby. "Hey, Reed," she adds, the words taking every ounce of her courage.

"Hi," he answers.

Their eyes meet briefly, but then Reed looks away. A sob rolls up Karyn's throat.

Reed looks at his watch. "We're gonna be late," he says.

Karyn looks from Reed to Shaheem, who seems confused by the sudden awkwardness between his friends.

"You're headed my way, aren't you, Dobi?" Reed says.

"Same as always," Shaheem answers. "See ya, Karyn."

Karyn gives him a small nod. She waits to see what Reed will do. Without another glance her way, he heads down the hall after Shaheem.

• • •

The bell rings Tuesday morning, signaling the end of homeroom. Jane sits up straight and looks around. The

119

other students lazily gather their stuff for first period. Nobody seems to have much energy this morning.

"Jane, I've got something for you," Mrs. Gormley says, holding up a thin white envelope. "Mrs. Carruthers dropped it off earlier."

Jane's pulse races. *Mrs. Carruthers. She finally got a record of my scores.* "Thanks, Mrs. Gormley," Jane says as she stands and reaches for her backpack.

She tries to imagine what her college guidance counselor will say about the scores. "There must be some mistake!" *No, Mrs. Carruthers, no mistake. 100 verbal, 100 math. That's as good as your prize student could do.*

Her body moves as though it's wading through molasses as she approaches Mrs. Gormley. How does she keep forgetting how many people she has to explain things to? At least a lot of the students have stopped asking about her scores, now that it's been about a week since theirs came and the topic of SATs is dying down. But a few of them, like Sumit, won't give up. And there's her parents, still waiting for an explanation. Now Mrs. Carruthers.

"Is everything okay, Jane?" Mrs. Gormley asks.

Jane looks at her teacher, remembering what she said to Jane in the courtyard yesterday. "I'm fine, Mrs. Gormley," Jane answers, taking the envelope. She stuffs it in her bag and hurries out of the classroom, starting down the hall. She'll read the note later. Right now she has to go pick up Peter for first period.

"Hi," she says when she sees Peter waiting outside his homeroom. "You've got History now, right?"

"Nope. Español," he says.

"God, I can't keep track of anything lately," she says.

Jane and Peter work their way through the halls in silence. She's gotten used to having him around, and in a strange way, it feels good. Before being assigned to help him, she'd never talked to anyone between classes. She raced through the hallways, and everyone around melted into a blur. Now things are slowing down, coming into focus—and it's all terrifying. Somehow she's beginning to really count on Peter's presence to keep things in perspective.

They're just turning down the foreign language hallway when Jane sees Mr. Bonnebaker, the Web site adviser.

"Hello, there," Mr. Bonnebaker says, looking from Peter to Jane. "We missed you yesterday."

Jane's hands make tight fists around the handlebars. He's referring to the Web site meeting that she blew off. She'd decided to bolt after school. Went home and took a nap. Of course, once she got home, she couldn't sleep since she felt so guilty about skipping the meeting. But that moment of actually leaving school on time had felt so good, even if the feeling didn't last.

She tries to come up with an excuse. She's got none. She clears her throat. "Sorry, Mr. Bonnebaker. I had this . . . uh, this thing for music and then I—"

"It's okay, Jane," Mr. Bonnebaker says with a smile. "I

just wanted to make sure everything was okay. If there's anyone who's on top of things, it's Jane Scott."

Jane chokes back a laugh.

He starts to walk away.

"Wait, Mr. Bonnebaker," she blurts out.

He turns back and looks at her. "Yes?"

"I . . . uh . . . I can't—"

"Oh, I almost forgot. The next meeting is tomorrow at three-thirty. Someone's coming in to help with the graphic design," Mr. Bonnebaker says before she can finish.

Jane swallows. "Mr. Bonnebaker, I can't do the Web site anymore," she says. "I quit." The words hang in the air. They're beautiful. They're horrifying.

"You what?" Mr. Bonnebaker exclaims after a second of silence. "You're the editor. The editor can't quit."

Can't quit. It's what she's always thought, that quitting was somehow impossible. That even if she wanted to, her mouth wouldn't be able to form those words and her voice wouldn't be able to pronounce them. But she was wrong. Of course she can quit. Nothing is really stopping her.

"I'm sorry. I thought I could handle it. But I've got a million responsibilities. I just can't do it. "

"Jane, would you please reconsider? People are depending on you. I'm depending on you."

Which is exactly why I have to quit. Jane shakes her head. "I'm sorry, Mr. B."

Mr. Bonnebaker glances at his watch. "I have to get to

class, but I hope we can discuss this later." He turns and walks down the hall. She watches him go, still stunned by how easy it was.

It's amazing, but it's true. Nothing is really stopping her at all.

• • •

Peter looks at Meena's back as she stares out the window of Dr. Lansky's office, waiting for her Tuesday afternoon appointment. He can barely make out her shoulders beneath the black wool sweater that hangs loosely to her waist. Her hair, which looks clean for once, is pulled back with a thin gold barrette. They haven't spoken since they arrived. Even during the car ride over, they barely talked— and not about anything real.

Hard rain splatters against the window, and Meena watches it like it's a movie.

What's she thinking? Peter wonders. *I wish she'd let her guard down. Just a little.*

"Are you going to say anything to him?" Peter risks the question, despite his promise to let the whole thing go for now.

She doesn't turn around. "What do you mean?"

"About Clayton. Are you gonna tell Dr. Lansky?"

Meena turns around. She looks so tired. "I told you everything is better now that he's gone."

Peter shakes his head. "You keep saying that, Meena, but I don't see it. You're not better."

123

Meena starts twisting her thumb ring. Peter has a sudden urge to rip that ring from her finger and throw it out the window, as if maybe then she'd finally talk freely.

"He—he asks so many questions," she says. "I just . . . I can't."

Peter nods, knowing he's not going to get anywhere. He takes a *National Geographic* from the end table and flips to a section on Antarctica. There's a picture of a massive ice floe drifting across a large body of water.

What if I'm the one who's supposed to say something? I'm the one she told. Well, sort of told. So am I doing the right thing keeping it quiet, or should I be telling someone who could help? Someone like his dad, the cop.

Peter feels a chill creep over him, remembering the last time he struggled over whether to tell his dad something. But that was so long ago. And it was totally different.

The door to Dr. Lansky's office opens and the doctor walks out, followed by Danny Chaiken. Peter does a double take. Freaky, seeing Danny here—and right when Peter was thinking about that day.

"Hello, Meena," Dr. Lansky says.

She nods a hello, then slides past him and Danny into the office. Dr. Lansky says good-bye to Danny, then steps in his office, shutting the door behind him.

"Hey, Peter," Danny says, digging his hands deep into his jeans pockets.

"Hey," Peter says.

124

"Don't tell me you're here to see the good ol' doctor, too?" Danny asks.

Peter smiles. "No. I'm just waiting for Meena. Not that I couldn't use some expert advice."

Danny shrugs. "Expert advice. I guess I need lots of that." He pauses, shooting Peter a cautious look. "But I guess that's obvious after what happened with Boyle."

Peter flashes back to the scene in history class. Boyle picking on him, pushing and pushing. And then Danny finally jumping up and shoving the guy into the wall. Peter had been so pissed. He didn't need one more person pitying him, fighting his battles for him because he's stuck in this chair.

"Look, I'm sorry about that," Danny says. "I know it looked like I was just being a jerk. I mean, I *was* just being a jerk. But it wasn't about you, you know?"

Peter nods. Gossip gets around at Falls High. Even enough to reach a guy in a wheelchair whose only real friends at the moment are the former school genius who is now apparently turning her back on it all, for some unknown reason, and a former popular girl who is no longer speaking to anyone in school but him, for a very horrifying reason. Peter knows that Danny was on some kind of medication, and when he stopped taking it, he lost control. He was even in a car accident after the Boyle thing. But obviously Danny's working on the problem if he's here at Lansky's office.

125

"Don't worry about it," Peter says. "I overreacted. Boyle's a creep, and you'd had enough. I guess I was just sick of everyone diving to even pick up a pen if I dropped it. I took it out on you."

Danny sinks down on the couch. "I think I know what you mean," he says. "It's different with me, but I still see the looks. Like they feel so bad for poor, crazy Danny. And some of them—some of them are even scared of me now, I think. It sucks just walking down the hall."

"The worst is the nervous glancers," Peter says. "You catch them giving you a quick look, all scared and pitying. Then they jerk their eyes away like you have Superman laser vision and you're going to burn them for looking at you."

"And then five seconds later they're staring at you again!" Danny shakes his head. "What's the matter with them?"

Peter laughs. "They're just idiots," he says. He puts the *National Geographic* back down the table. "It does get easier, though," he adds. "Dealing with the looks. They don't bug me as much anymore."

"That's good," Danny says.

They're quiet for a second, and Danny rubs his hands along his jeans. "So, you're here with Meena?"

"Uh-huh."

"Is she . . . okay?"

Peter shrugs. "There's some stuff going on with her."

"Stuff, hmm." Danny looks out the window, and his eyes glass over. Why is everyone so fascinated with that view? "I should get going," he finally says. "My mom's probably waiting outside."

"Yeah, okay," Peter says.

"But maybe . . . maybe I'll see you around?"

Peter's eyebrows rise. "Sure," he says.

Danny leaves, and Peter lets his own gaze drift to the rain outside. So strange, how they've all been around lately. Jane, Meena, Karyn, Reed, Jeremy, Danny . . . he wonders how much they think about what happened. Did it take them years to sleep through the night? Did they ever want to tell? Did any of them, when they heard about his accident, think what he thought when he woke up in that hospital and couldn't feel his legs? That finally he was being punished for what he'd done?

Peter frowns. What if it means something, all of them coming back into his life the way they have been? What if he really does have a shot at being forgiven?

• • •

Karyn lies on her bed Tuesday evening, staring at the ceiling. She's waiting for her father to pick her up for their pre-Thanksgiving celebration. *Why didn't I just say I'd take my own car? Then I could leave when I want. Now I'm going to be stuck there.*

The rain is still coming down as hard as it's been all day, and Karyn would give anything to curl up under her blankets and forget about the entire world. She groans and rolls over. Most likely her dad and Kelly will announce their

127

engagement at dinner. Karyn's stomach tightens at the thought of their two happy faces. About the only two happy faces in her life right now. What's she going to say when they tell her? All their marriage means to Karyn is that love is a total joke. Her dad stayed married to her mom for twenty years, then walked out when someone younger and prettier came along.

And her mom is stuck having a much harder time getting over her dad, which is so crazy since he's the one who's not even worth it. He's the one who couldn't hang in there when things were hard with her mom. The one who's shallow enough to actually want to marry *Kelly,* one of the most annoying and stupid women Karyn's ever met. So is that how love works? You just get hung up on the people who hurt you, and meanwhile they walk away totally fine? Smiling at their friends in the hallway like nothing's wrong?

Karyn blinks. No, Reed's not like her dad. He's nothing like him. But what if he is? She's sure her mom never thought her dad could be so harsh when they first fell in love and got married. And Karyn never would have imagined Reed could be so cold. So how can you ever know?

Karyn's gaze lands on the photo of her and T. J. in New York. It's not the best picture of her. The wind did serious damage to her hair. But she loves that shot of T. J. because he looks like he's about to burst from happiness. Just from being with her.

Karyn plays with the cuff of her brown turtleneck sweater. She can't do this anymore, can't keep going back and forth in her mind between Reed, T. J., Reed, T. J. It's like she's torn between two feelings, and she still doesn't even know what those feelings *are*. Does she love T. J.? Does she love Reed? Does she love *both* of them? Is that even possible?

She lets out a deep sigh, returning her focus to tonight and how she'll deal. She can picture the whole scene at their condo. Gourmet food. Classical music. Expensive wine. Halfway through dinner her father will make a toast. "Sweetheart, I have wonderful news. Kelly and I are . . ."

The doorbell rings. Footsteps. The front door opens and closes.

"Hello, Brian," Karyn hears her mom say in a distant, remote tone.

"Maggie."

Karyn's whole body goes cold. What if that's how she and Reed sound from now on? What if they never say more than that to each other again?

"Karyn," her mother calls, "your father is here."

Karyn lifts herself off the bed. Her legs are shaky as she heads down the stairs and into the foyer.

"Hi, sweetie," her father says.

"Hey, Dad," she says, kissing him on the cheek.

"Hungry?" he asks expectantly.

Karyn nods, then looks at her mother. The corners of her mom's mouth are tight, and her eyes can't seem to focus on anything. It's like she doesn't know what to do with herself. Karyn feels sick as she remembers that moment in the lobby with Reed this morning.

Mr. Aufiero holds Karyn's coat out to her, and she starts to slip it on.

Just then the doorbell rings again. Ms. Aufiero's head jerks in the direction of the door, then she quickly scoots past Karyn and her dad and swings open the door.

"Jake," she exclaims, her voice an octave higher than normal. "Perfect timing. I'm almost ready."

At the sight of the guy from yesterday morning, Karyn clenches her jaw, her hands, every inch of her body. *Almost ready for what?*

Jake nods to Mr. Aufiero and Karyn, his dark eyes shifting nervously. "I left the car running," he says.

Ms. Aufiero grabs her coat and wraps herself around Jake's arm, then leans up to give him a quick kiss on the lips.

It's terrible—totally humiliating. How could Karyn's mom let this guy pick her up right in front of her dad? And even *kiss* him in front of both of them?

And then it hits her—her mom did this on purpose. She timed it perfectly so that her dad would see Jake pick her up. *Don't you realize Dad doesn't care? You're just embarrassing yourself.*

"You remember Jake, don't you, honey?" her mom says, not meeting her gaze. As if that way she can pretend her daughter met this guy in some normal way, not half naked outside the bathroom in her own house.

Karyn's mouth drops open.

"I'm Brian Aufiero," Mr. Aufiero says, abruptly thrusting out a hand. "Karyn's father."

Jake gives Mr. Aufiero a shaky smile and returns the handshake.

"Brian, if you'd given me a minute, I would have introduced you," Ms. Aufiero says.

"Sorry, Maggie. I just wanted to make sure I know the people my daughter is being exposed to."

"Jake is not *people,* Brian. He's a man I'm dating," Ms. Aufiero says, tightening her grip around Jake.

Karyn fingers a button on her coat. This whole disgusting scene feels familiar in some horrible, very personal way that has nothing to do with her parents . . . a sick sense of déjà vu. But she can't get the reason why into focus.

"I apologize, Jake," Mr. Aufiero says. "You do understand my position. My daughter lives here, too."

Karyn's legs are still trembling. Unless she's actually perfectly still and it's the world around her that's shaking, about to crumble to pieces.

"How dare you speak to my guest this way," Ms. Aufiero says. "How dare you come to my house and act—"

"Act how, Maggie?" her father retorts. "Like a concerned parent? At least one of us should be."

The trembling grows stronger. Karyn wants to scream. She is suddenly surrounded by an earthquake and if she doesn't run, it will swallow her whole.

"Don't you *dare* criticize my parenting," Ms. Aufiero

131

bursts out. "This from the absentee father? Karyn and I are doing just fine, aren't we, sweetheart?"

Fine. You call this fine?

Instead of looking at her mom, Karyn looks at Jake. The only other person here who seems as embarrassed by all of this as she is.

"Karyn, honey, are you okay?" her mother asks.

She needs air. Needs to escape.

"I think I'd better go," Jake says.

"Don't go. I'm sorry you had to see this," Ms. Aufiero pleads.

"Really, Maggie. I'll give you a call soon," he says, wrenching his arm free.

Before her mother can say anything else, Jake is out the door. He doesn't even bother to pull it shut behind him.

"See what you've done, Brian?" her mother fumes.

"Oh, please, Maggie. Don't give me that."

Outside. I need to get outside. Karyn takes a small step toward the door. Then another. The cold November air brushes against her skin. She hears the rain, sees it pouring down on her front step. Her parents continue to fight, but she can no longer process their voices. All she wants is quiet. A place where she doesn't feel like her life is being pulled apart.

Before she realizes what she's doing, she's shoving past her parents and rushing out the front door. The sky is a deep, dark gray. Karyn heads for the woods, her legs picking up speed with each step. And this time, she knows full well where she's headed—to Peter Davis's house.

CHAPTER EIGHT

I can't keep *surprising him like this,* Karyn thinks as she stands outside Peter's bedroom window.

Peter sits hunched over his desk, reading a book, just like the last time she was here. Karyn almost doesn't want to disturb him. There's this incredible calmness surrounding him. It's why she came back tonight—because of what she felt when she was here yesterday. She has no idea what it is, but there's just something so warm and soothing about Peter and this room.

Cautiously, she lifts a finger to the glass and taps.

Peter turns his head. He doesn't even flinch.

"I'm sorry," she mouths.

Peter wheels himself over to the window and lets her in.

"You must be freezing," he says, eyeing her dripping clothes. She looks down at herself. Her boots are caked with mud.

"I'll try not to make a mess," she says. But it's no use. His rug is already splattered with mud.

133

"Don't worry about it," he says. "Let me get you a towel."

When he leaves, Karyn takes off her shoes. She wiggles her cramped toes. *Bad idea to go running in my boots.* Next she removes her coat and holds it in her lap. She may be chilled to the bone, but it's nothing compared to what she was feeling minutes ago in her house. She looks around the dim, neat room. The only light comes from a desk lamp, which gives off a soft whitish glow. Not too intense, just mellow. Karyn wishes she could curl up in a tiny ball and fit inside the space where the light falls.

"Here you go," Peter says, coming back in the room and tossing her a towel.

"Thanks," she says, rubbing it through her hair.

Peter wheels back over to his desk while Karyn dries herself off. No questions. Karyn places the towel on a chair by the window and sits down. Peter looks up at her and gives her a reassuring smile.

"I feel pretty stupid," Karyn admits quietly.

"Don't worry about it," Peter answers. "Use the blanket," he says, pointing to the same blanket he offered her yesterday morning. It's draped over the back of his chair, just where she left it.

Karyn wraps the heavy blanket around her shoulders. "I know I owe you an explanation, but I don't . . . I just . . ." She stops, unsure of what else to say.

"Like I said, don't worry," Peter says. "Just relax. I'm

gonna go ahead and keep reading my history chapter. Boyle is such a hard-ass about putting students on the spot."

"Yeah, that's what I've heard," Karyn says.

Peter hunches back over his book.

Karyn pulls her legs to her chest. She knew somehow that Peter would understand exactly what she needs right now, even though they barely know each other anymore. He gets that she doesn't want to talk. But she doesn't want to be alone, either. She just wants to be with someone who doesn't make her feel hurt, or angry, or guilty.

Why would you marry someone you don't love? But her dad must have loved her mom once, as hard as it is to believe after seeing them talk to each other the way they just did. She can remember, when she was young, there were times when her dad would bring home flowers for her mom for no reason. Or her parents would just exchange a glance across the kitchen table and both get these funny smiles on their faces, like they had a private world of things only the other understood.

Like what Jeremy had said about her and Reed.

Karyn closes her eyes and takes a few long breaths. Suddenly she knows what that scene with Jake and her parents was reminding her of—the disaster with Tim Cavanaugh in the cafeteria yesterday. She'd been just as pathetic as her mom, flirting with Tim to get Reed's attention. And Reed had only been disgusted by her, like her dad's disgusted by her mom. Like *she's* disgusted by her mom.

So that's it then, isn't it? How can Reed be the right person for her if he makes her act like such a fool? She can't imagine ever doing something so dumb with T. J. Because she knows how T. J. feels about her—she trusts it. She trusts *him*.

More than anything, T. J. makes her feel safe. She misses the way his arms encircle her. Squeeze her. The way they never let go. Karyn pulls the blanket tighter. She thinks about her mom's arms around Jake. Clinging. Desperate. She never wants to feel like that, be like that with someone.

"Everything okay?" Peter asks, looking up from his book.

Karyn nods. "Better."

She thinks about T. J.'s invitation for this weekend. Why has she been so hesitant? Seeing him is just what she needs. *That's it, Karyn, you're going. No more doubts. He's the one.*

• • •

Wednesday morning, Jane Scott walks to her music theory class, humming to herself. She thinks of all the things she should have done last night. Practice her sax. Prepare for the next Academic Decathlon meet. Study AP French. Study the SAT books her dad bought so she'd be prepared for the retake. *Yes, I should have done all of those things, but I didn't do a single one. What would Mom and Dad say if they knew I spent over an hour trying to count the raindrops that hit my window?*

Her parents aren't the only ones who would be shocked,

disappointed, confused to know that. Jane finally read the note from Mrs. Carruthers when she got home yesterday. There were no real surprises. Mrs. Carruthers went on about Jane's *potential*, how she doesn't understand what happened with the SATs. Wants to talk about what they can do, how they can keep this from ruining Jane's chances of getting into college. When, of course, there's nothing anyone can do. Not really.

"Jane, wait up."

She stops short just before entering the classroom and sees Danny Chaiken walking toward her, wearing baggy cargo pants and a light brown T-shirt with some crazy design. "Hey, Danny. What's up?"

"Where have you been?" he asks.

"Around," Jane says casually.

"Around? What about band practice? You missed the last two and Vega was worried."

Jane feels a familiar twinge of guilt and fear mixed together. Mr. Vega counts on her. He'll be upset, want an explanation. What's she going to tell him?

Then she slows down her breathing and reminds herself that it doesn't matter—none of this matters anymore. It's getting a little easier each day. Jane thinks of what Peter said to her. *He's right. Becoming a slacker does take hard work.* Even with the voice in her head telling her that she's done being what everyone else wants her to be, done trying to live her parents' dreams, she still feels a constant buzz of noise—thoughts about everything she's not doing and everything she's lost. Her entire future, down the drain.

She clears her throat. "Sorry, Danny. I guess . . . I guess I spaced. I'm sure Mr. Vega—"

"You spaced? How can you space rehearsal? We're doing the Charlie Parker piece. The one *you* picked out. The one where you have a three-minute solo!"

She looks him right in the eye, resisting the urge to let autopilot guilty Jane take over. She remembers how she spent the afternoon in the nurse's office when Danny told her he hadn't written her audition piece for college. What was the point?

"I forgot, Danny. What else can I say?"

He stares back at her, his eyes bugging out in surprise. He's never heard her talk like that. No one has.

Jane keeps walking into the classroom, leaving Danny to deal with his shock. She spots an empty desk by the window. Forget front and center. Jane wants to know what it's like to fade into the background. Changing her seat will be part of her new attitude. *Slackers always sit in the back. Peter would be proud!*

Mr. Vega strides into the room, and Jane digs around her backpack, keeping her head down. It's one thing not to let a guilt trip from Danny work, but Mr. Vega is another story. He even volunteered his free time to help her with her audition tape. And this is how she pays him back? By skipping rehearsals.

"Hello, Jane," he says as he approaches her desk.

"Hi, Mr. Vega." *Please let this be easy.*

"Is there something you want to tell me?" Mr. Vega asks. He crosses his arms in front of his chest.

Jane shifts uncomfortably. *I know I let him down. But he has no idea how many other people are counting on me, too.*

"I'm sorry I missed practice, Mr. Vega," she says. "I've been really busy."

He nods. "Jane, is there anything I can help you with? Did you get your applications out to the conservatories okay?"

A hot flush crawls up Jane's neck. *Why does he have to be so nice?* "No, I didn't."

His brow furrows. "Jane, is everything all right?"

She looks down at her desk. *It's time he knows I'm a failure. Maybe I should start a club—the Who's Been Let Down by Jane Scott Club.*

Jane takes a deep breath and begins to speak in a measured tone. "Mr. Vega, it's about band. . . . I don't have time. . . . You probably should find someone else to fill my spot."

"What? Jane, you can't be serious," he says loud enough for a few people to turn and look.

Her head starts to spin. First Bonnebaker and the Web site. Now Mr. Vega. She can't believe she's had the nerve to do this two days in a row. Jane grips her desk for balance.

"You're our key sax player!" he exclaims.

Jane keeps her eyes focused on the graffiti. "Sorry, Mr. Vega."

"What about all the work you've put in?" he asks.

What about it? I only did it for you, my parents, the rest of the band. I never did it for myself.

"I'm sorry, Mr. Vega. But I really need to take a break."

The bell rings.

"Jane, we should talk about this later," Mr. Vega says. He turns and walks to the front of the classroom.

When he's gone, Jane realizes her knuckles are white from gripping the desk so tightly.

• • •

Reed grabs his sneakers and a clean pair of socks out of his gym locker, then sinks down on the bench and starts to put them on. It's one o'clock on Wednesday afternoon, and the school is nearly empty because of early dismissal for Thanksgiving break. But Reed didn't feel like going home just yet. He couldn't face the prospect of sitting in his house, thinking about . . .

Can't he get her out of his mind for ten minutes? Five?

It would help if he didn't have so many emotions battling it out for first place, too. How can he be furious at Karyn and completely in love with her at the same time? One part of him can't get past how Karyn could treat T. J. so badly—acting like she doesn't even *have* a boyfriend. But none of that makes sense in his mind with the Karyn he knows better than anyone else in the world. The Karyn he loves more than anyone else in the world.

Reed ties his shoelaces and jumps up, heading for the weight room. He's kind of relieved that Jeremy couldn't stick around—he's not up for more of his friend's grilling. Jeremy's taking his little sister, Emily, out to lunch. He wanted to do something special for her since he won't be home for Thanksgiving tomorrow. *I can't believe the Mandiles haven't asked Jeremy to come home. Not even for Thanksgiving. I wonder when that stalemate is going to end?*

Reed gives the door to the locker room a frustrated shove and enters the weight room, expecting it to be empty. But there's someone in here already—Peter Davis. He's sitting in his wheelchair with his back to Reed, lifting a pair of weights over his head. He's so focused on lifting, he doesn't even notice Reed.

Reed waits for Peter to finish his set, then walks over to him. "Hey, how's the workout going?" he asks.

Peter turns to face him, and Reed sees the sweat pouring down the sides of his face. He's really pushing himself.

"Pretty good," Peter answers, exchanging his weights for a heavier pair. "Didn't hear you come in."

"You're really hard-core," Reed says, lifting a pair of thirty pounders from the weight rack.

"Gotta be," Peter says, gesturing to his legs. He grunts as he brings the weights down. "I can't believe you guys do this for fun."

"I wouldn't really call it fun," Reed says as he exhales. "More like necessary."

"Necessary for what? Self-inflicted torture?"

Reed laughs. "Coach says we should lift every other day.

141

Sometimes I do it 'cause I need to. Takes the edge off, you know."

Peter grabs a towel and wipes the sweat from his brow. "Goes either way for me. Sometimes it puts the edge *on*."

"Like I said, if you need any help, I'm here," Reed says.

"Thanks."

Reed and Peter work out in silence, occasionally letting out groans from exertion. Reed can't get over Peter's determination. It actually helps Reed focus, keeps him from getting too stuck in his head.

"You got any plans this weekend?" Reed asks when the two take a break between sets.

Peter reaches for his water bottle. "Not really. Maybe a movie with Meena."

"Meena Miller," Reed says with a smile. "I see you guys together all the time."

"Not all the time," Peter says casually.

"What's up with her? She's gone MIA. I heard she even dropped off the swim team."

Peter shrugs. "Going through some stuff, I guess."

"Must be major stuff. Last week Karyn told me she was worried about her. She's pretty much dropped all her friends."

Peter presses his fingers into his palms to crack his knuckles. "She told me she'd had enough of the cool crowd. Wanted to join the slacker crowd," he says with a smirk.

Reed frowns, not sure how to reply. It's pretty obvious Peter knows something, but it's not Reed's business.

"Can you spot me for this last set?" Peter asks. "My arms are beat."

"No problem." Reed gets up and walks behind Peter.

Peter raises his arms, holding the dumbbells on either side of his body. He pushes upward, doing the first six reps on his own. By the seventh, he's panting loudly. Reed places his hands under Peter's upper arms, helping him through the final reps.

Reed feels good that he's finally helping. Finally doing something more worthwhile than wallowing in his own melodrama. ". . . ten, eleven, twelve. You got it, man. Nice job."

Peter drops the weights to the floor. "Thanks."

Reed nods and sits back down on his bench. He pauses. *Here I am falling apart, and this guy is so together.*

It's nice hanging around someone who's got things so clear in his head. Reed's been wondering if he and Jeremy living together isn't the greatest thing right now, with them both going through so much crap. Reed likes the way he and Peter can just be here together, lifting weights, not talking about anything serious.

Reed looks at Peter in the mirror. "Hey, did you hear about Faith Saunders's party Friday night?"

"Yeah. Her parents are in Europe, right?"

"Yep. Maybe you should stop by. Her parties are known to last until sunrise."

Peter looks down at his legs. "It's been a while since I've been to a party."

143

"It'll be cool. That is, of course, unless *you're* beyond the cool crowd, too," Reed says.

Peter laughs. "Sunrise, huh?"

"Sunrise."

• • •

Karyn drops her backpack in the front hall Wednesday afternoon and tosses her coat over a chair. Every muscle in her body aches. She had stayed at Peter's house pretty late last night, trudging back through the cold, wet woods at close to midnight. When she got home, she saw her mother's light shining beneath her bedroom door. She'd probably waited up until Karyn got home. But she knew better than to open that door. Karyn knew that her mom wouldn't have wanted to hear anything her daughter had to say.

Right now, there are three things on Karyn's mind. *Hot tea. A warm blanket. A soft bed.* She hasn't felt right all day, and she knows if she doesn't take care of herself, she's going to get sick. And then she can kiss her weekend with T. J. good-bye. And that's the last thing she wants now that she's made her decision. It's time to put Reed behind her once and for all. Time to get closer to T. J.

So the only question is . . . how close?

Karyn sucks in a nervous breath. She knows that T. J. is the right guy for her, the one she wants to be with, but it's still so hard to imagine losing her virginity to him. *No, not hard—scary.* Isn't everyone scared to have sex for the first time, even if they don't all admit it?

Karyn walks into the kitchen, her thoughts far away in Boston. She stops dead when she sees her mother sitting at the kitchen table, an old photo album open in front of her. The garage door had been closed when Karyn got home, and she parked in the driveway, so she hadn't known if her mother's car was here or not. But she'd figured her mom was at the faculty meeting she saw the other teachers heading to after the students were dismissed early.

"Mom?"

Ms. Aufiero doesn't look up from the photo album, and Karyn realizes she's crying, very softly.

"Mom?" she says. "Are you okay?"

"Hi, sweetie," her mother says, her voice cracking. "I'm fine."

Karyn walks over and stands behind her mother, then looks down at the photos. Wedding photos. Karyn hasn't seen them in years.

"Mom, what are you doing this for?" Karyn asks, pulling up a chair.

"Look at this one." Her mother points to a black-and-white shot where she's feeding her father wedding cake. Both of their mouths are covered in frosting. "Do you think he ever remembers how happy we were?"

Karyn's heart sinks. Her mother's eyes are red and puffy—she's obviously been crying for a while. *Why is she torturing herself? Why can't she see that if he's actually enough of a jerk to ditch us in the first place, then replace us with Kelly in less than a year, he doesn't deserve either of our love?*

145

"I'm sure he remembers, Mom. But come on, you can't do this. He's not worth it." Karyn doesn't know what else to say. She's been so angry at her mom, so disgusted and horrified by everything she's done. But deep down she gets it—she's seen how close she came to being just as pathetic, just as desperate. And how can she hate her mom for not being strong enough to beat it when Karyn herself isn't convinced that *she* can?

"You're right, honey. You're absolutely right." Ms. Aufiero quickly shuts the photo album and pushes it away. "I'm so sorry about last night. I—I don't even know what I'm doing anymore."

Karyn stares at the beautiful photo album lying closed on the table. She has an urge to grab it and run into the other room to throw it in the fireplace. It doesn't seem right that the album should be so perfect and pretty when her parents' marriage was just the opposite.

Her mother reaches for a tissue from the box on her lap. "When I see your father and I think of him marrying that . . . that woman, it makes me crazy. Karyn, you have to believe me—I never really thought he and I could end up like this." She raises her gaze to meet Karyn's, and her red eyes are pleading. "I'm sorry I let this happen to your family, sweetie. It's not fair—not fair for you."

Karyn fights not to cry. "No, Mom, it's—I'm sorry. About last night. I shouldn't have run off like that."

Ms. Aufiero lets out a sob. "You have nothing to be

sorry about, Karyn, *nothing.* You're my daughter, and you shouldn't have to—this shouldn't be happening to you. You should be out shopping with your friends, having fun, not watching your mother fall apart. I promise, sweetie. I promise I'll change."

Karyn's eyes shine with tears. "I just wish you were okay," she says. Without thinking, she leans over and sinks into her mother's arms, holding on to her as tightly as she can.

Ms. Aufiero squeezes back, pressing her close, and the warmth of her tears soaks through Karyn's shirt.

She says she'll change, but Karyn has trouble buying it. Not because her mom is a liar. And not because she's a slut. No, it's because she *can't* change. It's too late. All her strength left when her husband walked out. And how can Karyn blame her for that?

Ms. Aufiero pulls away and kisses Karyn on the cheek. "I love you, Karyn. Things get so"—she pauses to blow her nose—"they just get so hard. I promise I'll make it better."

"Okay, Mom," Karyn says. She's not going to argue, not going to protest that she knows it's not true. That's not what her mom needs. And it's not what Karyn needs, either.

Karyn knows what she can do, for both of them. She can make sure that she does whatever she has to do to never end up sitting in that kitchen chair, crying over a man who doesn't want her.

CHAPTER NiNE

"It's a good thing your great-aunt Betsy isn't here to see this," Ms. Aufiero says, opening a packet of soy sauce.

Karyn laughs. She hadn't minded at all when her mom asked if they could scrap the usual turkey fare and order out from The Cottage instead. It's not like today feels like a real Thanksgiving, anyway.

"She'd probably figure we were headed straight to hell for not eating a turkey," Karyn says.

"I hope you're not disappointed, honey. I figured since it was just the two of us, we should do something different."

"Are you kidding?" Karyn says, loading her plate with rice. "I'm always up for The Cottage. If we feel like a turkey next week, we can have it then."

"Absolutely!"

Karyn is relieved that her mom seems much better than yesterday. She'd heard her crying most of the night through her bedroom door, and it had made it pretty hard to sleep. Especially since Karyn's own mind was racing—she couldn't stop thinking about this weekend with T. J. Because she knows now, she knows what she's going to do. What she has to do.

She lay there wide awake, listening to all the voices in her head—her mom talking about taking sex seriously, Gemma babbling about Carlos and lingerie, T. J. telling her he loves her over and over again. She's been so confused about sex and love and how they fit together. But now she gets it—sex can only bring you closer if you're both in love. And that's her and T. J. So all she has to do is get over her silly fear and do it, and then she'll be certain that she loves him as much as he loves her.

"By the way, how's Jeremy Mandile doing these days? Is he home for Thanksgiving?" Ms. Aufiero asks.

Karyn shakes her head. "His parents haven't asked him to come home. He's spending Thanksgiving with the Frasiers."

"It sounds like he's going to have it tough for a while."

Tough is an understatement. Jeremy acts like he's fine, but she knows it's not true. Even if she couldn't see for herself, Reed's told her how upset Jeremy looks when certain things come up over dinner, comments about family stuff.

At least, that's what Reed told her when they were still actually talking to each other.

"Any more dumplings?" her mom asks.

Karyn passes her mom the container and leans back in her chair. The next few moments pass in silence except for her mother's chopsticks clicking against her plate. Suddenly the idea of Chinese food on Thanksgiving seems overwhelmingly sad. She imagines Reed's table. There are a few occasions

149

when Mrs. Frasier actually cooks, instead of just ordering in gourmet food. Every year on Thanksgiving, she cooks. Karyn knows Mr. Frasier was a Thanksgiving junkie. Wanted everything to be perfect. So Reed and T. J. have sort of carried it on since their father died.

Karyn feels a slight tug in her chest. Reed hasn't called today. The two of them have a ritual of calling each other on major holidays and sharing tidbits about crazy stuff their families are doing. Last year had been especially helpful since Karyn's parents had been engaged in a screaming match to end all screaming matches.

It doesn't matter. Things are different now. This time tomorrow, I'll be on my way to Boston. Oh my God. This time Saturday, I'll no longer be a virgin. Karyn takes a deep breath.

"Did you eat too fast, honey?" her mom asks. "You don't look so good."

Karyn exhales. "I'm fine."

"What do you say we rent a movie? We can pick up ice cream and make sundaes," Karyn's mom says eagerly.

"Can we do it a little later?" Karyn asks. "I promised Amy Santisi I'd stop by this afternoon so we could work on a new cheer. We want it ready for the Kennedy game."

"On Thanksgiving?" her mother says.

"Yeah, Amy has to go away with her family tomorrow. I promise it won't take more than a few hours."

"That's fine, sweetie. I understand," her mom says, obviously trying not to sound too disappointed—and failing.

150

"Are you sure, Mom? I can cancel."

"Of course I'm sure," Ms. Aufiero says. "I'm proud of you for working so hard. I'll take a nap, and by the time you get home, I'll be ready for dessert."

Karyn stands up and brings her dishes to the sink. "The Santisis eat early, so I'll go over now," Karyn says, rinsing off the plates. "I'll pick up a few movies on my way home. Any preferences?"

"Nothing too gory," her mom answers.

"No problem," Karyn says, then shuts off the faucet and hurries upstairs to her bedroom to grab a sweater. Karyn's cell phone sits on her dresser. She notices that the message light is blinking, and her heart does an excited flip.

She stares at the phone a second, then grabs it and quickly types in her password, holding her breath as she waits to hear the message.

"Hi, honey, it's your dad."

Karyn sinks down onto her bed, feeling like she's been punched in the stomach. Stupid. Why would Reed call her when he obviously hates her now?

"I wanted to wish you a happy Thanksgiving," her dad continues on the message. "I'm so sorry about the other night. Please let me make it up to you. Kelly has planned another dinner. Call me so we can make a date. By the way, we have some big news."

Karyn reaches up to rub her temple. Does he actually believe that Karyn is going to be happy for him? You can't just walk out on your family and find a new one like that.

Karyn tosses the phone in her bag. She wishes it were tomorrow already. Suddenly she can't wait until it's just her and T. J., and she can make the rest of the world disappear.

• • •

Jane sits in the passenger seat next to her mother Thursday afternoon as they drive on the quiet back roads to her aunt's house for Thanksgiving dinner. The heat in the car is on full blast and Jane feels the air slowly drain the moisture from her skin.

"You seem a lot more relaxed, dear," her mom says.

"I guess," Jane replies blandly.

"I'm sure it's because of what we talked about. You just needed to drop some of those extracurriculars. Focus on what really matters to you—your music."

Jane wishes the car were stopped at a light. If it were, she'd get out. She'd walk in any direction she felt like. As long as it was far away from her mother's voice.

"Don't you agree?"

Jane nods so her mother has to turn her head. Couldn't she please, for a single day, not talk about school?

"I'm sorry, Jane, but I just can't stop thinking about all the pressure your father was putting on you—it was too much. The constant talk of Ivy Leagues. Yale this. Harvard that." She pauses. "And I know—I know it was my fault, too."

"What?" Jane gives her mother her full attention, her heart thumping in her chest.

"Well, of course. I mean, I saw what he was doing to you. I should have made more of an effort to stop it, to keep him from piling so much work on you."

Jane's hopes sink. Of course that's what her mom meant. Of course it all still comes down to blaming her dad.

"Mom," Jane begins. She's about to tell her that it was *both* her parents' expectations that drove her over the edge. But the words catch in her throat. *I can't fight them anymore. It's too tiring. They don't listen.*

"What is it?" her mom asks.

"Nothing." Jane leans her head against the window. She zones out on the double yellow line in the middle of the road. Just a few hours ago, she ate Thanksgiving lunch with her father. Their conversation had been very similar. "I'm so glad you decided to drop band. Your mother means well, I'm sure, but band is distracting you from what's important."

Jane sinks into the seat.

"Maybe we can spend next Thanksgiving in New York," her mom says. "I've never taken a carriage ride through Central Park. Wouldn't that be fun?"

Jane doesn't answer. The heat is unbearable. Her mom just keeps talking about New York. Jane cracks the window.

Quitting the Web site and band had been totally liberating. So had telling Danny Chaiken she didn't care and slacking off on her homework. The only thing getting her undivided attention these days is TCBY. *I should feel better, right?*

So why does she still feel trapped? Why can't she look at

her parents and say, "I quit," just like she did with Mr. Vega and Mr. Bonnebaker?

• • •

White candles flicker around the Frasier dining room, casting shadows on the walls. Reed is sitting down to Thanksgiving dinner with his mother, grandparents, and Jeremy. Classical music plays softly on the stereo. Even though it's a small group, Reed's mom insisted everyone dress up. Reed wasn't too psyched to wear a tie, but he did, anyway. He knows how upset she is about T. J. not being here.

Although, judging from the food on the table, you'd never know T. J. wasn't showing. Mrs. Frasier cooked all his favorite food. For dessert there's even a raspberry-rhubarb pie. Reed hates rhubarb. He likes pumpkin pie better, but his mother said it would make her feel better to serve T. J.'s favorites.

"How's football going, Reed?" his grandfather asks.

Reed cracks a smile as he glances at his grandfather's bow tie and vest. He still dresses the way he did when he was an English professor at Columbia University.

"I'm playing pretty well this year," Reed answers, looking down at his plate. "But nothing to make the headlines."

"Are you kidding me?" Jeremy chimes in. "Reed's doing awesome. His sprint is about to break every record."

Reed flashes Jeremy a warning look. He doesn't want any references to breaking records. That would mean breaking T. J.'s records. Which would mean breaking Mrs. Frasier's heart. Reed takes a sip of red wine, savoring the tartness of it.

"More turkey, anyone?" Mrs. Frasier asks.

"I'd love some, Mrs. Frasier," Jeremy says.

"I imagine our record breaker here would like something substantial," Reed's grandfather says, giving Reed a wink. For some reason his superintellectual grandfather has this romantic notion about having two athletic grandsons.

Reed shakes his head. "I'm stuffed."

"Don't the scouts come around about now?" his grandfather presses.

Reed nods. "I heard a rumor that they're coming by soon. But who knows?" A lie. The scouts are a huge deal and Reed knows exactly when they'll be around. There are a few coming to this Saturday's game, in fact. Including the scout from Boston College.

"Well, that sounds very exciting," Reed's grandmother says. "Maybe you and T. J. can play together at BC."

"I don't think Reed has football in mind when it comes to college, Mom," Mrs. Frasier says as she passes the platter of turkey around the table.

Reed nods stiffly. He drains his wine. When he refills his glass, he catches Jeremy watching him. *What? It's a glass of wine. Give me a break.*

"We should give T. J. a call after dinner," Reed's mom says. "The poor thing is going out to some restaurant with the team. It doesn't sound too festive."

The poor thing is probably doing funnels in some nasty frat house.

155

"A colleague from Boston said he read about T. J. in the *Boston Herald*," his grandfather says. "Apparently he's making quite an impression. Not bad for a freshman."

"Reed, you and I are going to have to go there for a game soon," Mrs. Frasier says.

"Sounds good," Reed answers without much enthusiasm. Mrs. Frasier rarely makes it to Reed's games and he plays in the same town. Why is it so hard to acknowledge that both of her sons are good at football? Why is it so hard to acknowledge anything that Reed does?

He gulps down most of his second glass of wine. No one at the table seems to be noticing, so why not?

"How's Karyn doing these days?" his grandmother asks. "It's so wonderful that she and T. J. have managed to stay together. Long distance can be trying on a relationship, especially with two people so young."

"Karyn's doing great," Jeremy says quickly. He gives Reed a sideways glance. "Still, you know, cheerleading and stuff."

Reed wraps his hand around the stem of the wineglass. The delicate crystal feels weak in his hand. Karyn. What's she doing today? He has no idea.

"T. J. says she's driving to Boston tomorrow," Mrs. Frasier adds. "I'm glad. It'll cheer him up."

Reed feels the wine crawl back up his throat. *I didn't think she'd go. Not after what happened. So what does that mean? Are they together the same as before? Is she even going to tell him what happened?*

156

Reed's fingers tighten around the glass. The memory of Karyn's lips against his morphs into an image of her kissing his brother, and for a second he thinks he's going to be sick. *No, she doesn't love T. J. I saw it in her eyes. I felt it in that kiss. Stop . . . no, I'm wrong. Obviously I'm wrong.*

The phone rings, and Reed jumps. He drops the wineglass and red wine fans out across the tablecloth.

"Nobody touch it," Mrs. Frasier exclaims. "I'll get some salt to soak up the stain." She jumps up from the table and rushes into the kitchen.

The phone continues to ring.

"Hello?" he hears his mother say.

Reed holds his breath. *Karyn.* They have a tradition of calling each other every holiday. They had a tradition.

"Jeremy," Reed's mother calls. "It's Emily."

Jeremy's face breaks into a grin, and he pushes back his chair and hurries into the kitchen.

Of course. Of course it's Emily.

Mrs. Frasier comes out with some salt and pours it on the wine stain.

"Sorry, Mom," Reed says.

Mrs. Frasier shrugs. "Just a tablecloth." She picks up the wine bottle sitting in front of him. "But why don't I put this on my end of the table."

Reed nods.

Of course it's not Karyn. And suddenly he feels emptier than he's ever felt in his life.

CHAPTER TEN

Karyn Aufiero heads out on the New York State Thruway Friday morning, listening to David Gray on the radio. She opens the window a crack to let in some cool air. Rolling hills stretch out on either side, interrupted by occasional farmhouses. She takes in the beautiful view. Soon the landscape will turn white with snow.

She drums her fingers on the steering wheel, filled with nervous energy. She hasn't been able to sit still in the last twenty-four hours. Pretty soon she'll be in Boston, with T. J. She'll look him in the eye and tell him he's the one she wants to be with. And he'll know how much she loves him. Enough to lose her virginity to him. She's ready.

She's done with silly fantasies, and she's done fooling herself that Reed is the one she wants. *T. J.* loves her, and T. J. is the guy she's meant to be with.

Karyn remembers the sight of her mom curled up in front of the television when she got home from Amy Santisi's last night. As promised, Karyn had gone to the video store and rented two movies. *Thelma & Louise* because Karyn is a Brad Pitt junkie and a new release with Harrison Ford, Ms. Aufiero's favorite. They had watched both, but Karyn's mind was miles away. She was sitting across from T. J. at a romantic restaurant. Candles flickered between them. He leaned across the table and kissed her forehead. Her lips.

Boston. 190 miles.

Karyn's heart leaps when she sees the large green sign on the side of the highway. *You'd better start paying attention to the road, or you'll never make it to Boston.*

Karyn lets out a nervous giggle. She can't stop imagining what tonight will be like. Maybe they'll dance a little. Walk through Faneuil Hall. T. J. had taken her there on her last visit. She loves the old brick buildings and the lights that look a century old.

I wonder if Mom wishes she could have a first time again? A fresh start.

Karyn clutches the wheel. When will she tell him that she's ready to have sex? Should she tell him at all or just guide him in that direction? She doesn't want it to feel forced. It should just happen. That's the way it's supposed to be when things are right.

Karyn turns the volume on the radio a notch higher. This is the biggest day of her life. No more wondering which Frasier brother is right for her. She's made her decision, and she knows it's the right one.

● ● ●

"Enjoy," Jane says, handing a peanut butter cone to an anxious kid.

"Say thank you," his mother advises.

The boy looks at Jane, his mouth already covered with frozen yogurt. "Thanks," he mutters.

Jane gives him a slight you're-welcome nod.

TCBY isn't very busy for a Friday afternoon. Everyone's probably still stuffed from Thanksgiving. Jane crosses her arms and leans against the counter. Reed leisurely wipes down tables on the other side of the store. She likes working her shifts with him. The two of them spend a lot of time complaining about work, but the truth is, Jane doesn't mind it much. It's easy. Brainless. All you have to do is serve the yogurt.

She picks up a rag and wipes up a blob of chocolate sauce from the counter. *It wouldn't be so bad to do this for the rest of my life. Customers barely notice you when you serve them. All they expect from you is yogurt.*

The bell above the door rings and Jane looks up. Peter Davis is being wheeled in the store by his father. "Hey, what's up?" Peter says, smiling at her.

"Not much," Jane answers.

"Hey, Peter," Reed calls from the other side of the store. "Never see you here." He walks over to Jane.

"Yeah, I'm a real ice cream person," Peter says with a shrug. "None of this artificial stuff. But my dad's a fan. He just picked me up from physical therapy, right around the corner."

"Jane. Reed. Nice to see you both," Mr. Davis says.

"Did you have a good Thanksgiving, Mr. Davis?" Jane asks.

"Yes, my wife cooked up a storm," he says, stepping up to the counter and examining the flavor selections. "I'd like an extra-large white chocolate mousse," he says after a moment.

"Sure," Jane replies. She takes a cone and walks over to the frozen yogurt machine.

"What'd you decide about tonight?" she hears Reed ask Peter.

"I'll definitely try and make it," Peter replies. "It's just that I—I should check with Meena first."

"Well, it should be something," Reed says. "Faith Saunders's parties always are."

"Sounds like a good time," Mr. Davis chimes in. "I can drop you off," he tells Peter.

"Or I could give you a ride," Reed adds.

Jane pulls the lever down on the machine and the yogurt fills the cone. She'd forgotten all about that party. Reed had mentioned it to her last week, when he gave her a ride home after she passed out. She hadn't thought of actually going, though. She just isn't someone who goes to parties. And at the time, her life was in the middle of falling apart—and she still thought she could somehow stop it from happening. But everything's changed now, hasn't it? And this isn't just any party. Faith is Quinn Saunders's little sister—so if she goes, she could see where Quinn grew up. Yeah, that crush was a long time ago, but she's still pretty curious. . . .

Jane hands Mr. Davis his cone. "Here you go."

"Thanks, Jane," he answers.

"You know, I was trying to get Jane to come, too," Reed tells Peter.

"Really? You're thinking of coming?" Peter says, looking at her with raised eyebrows.

Jane shakes her head, more as a reflex.

"Come on," Peter says. "You should."

"I'm not exactly in the same crowd as Faith Saunders, if you didn't notice," she says.

Peter laughs. "And I am?" he asks. Jane cracks a smile. "Besides," he adds. "What about your commitment to becoming a slacker?"

Jane looks back and forth between Reed and Peter. These guys actually want to hang out with her, at a party. It feels good. And isn't that what she's all about now— doing what *she* wants to do?

"Okay, yeah," she says, feeling a rush of excitement. "I'll go."

• • •

Early Friday evening, Peter sits in his room and dials Meena's number. He knows they didn't have real plans for tonight, but he still feels like he should check with her about this party. In case she needs him. Still, selfishly he can't help hoping she'll tell him it's fine. Now that he's done with the only real friends he had, he could use the chance to make some new ones. Ones that don't get high all day.

The phone rings, and he leans back in his chair.

He can't even remember the last time he went to a party. Sometime before the accident. It's one thing seeing a guy in a wheelchair around school . . . but what about at a party? How will everyone act?

"Hello?" a male voice says.

Clayton. What's he doing there? I thought he moved out. Peter's hands clench into fists. Then he remembers what Meena said, about her brothers being home for the Thanksgiving break, and he lets out a relieved sigh. It could be Meena's father, too. Why does his brain keep going right to worst-case scenarios?

"Hey, is Meena there?" he says.

"Sure, hold on. Meena! Telephone."

After a few moments he hears someone fumbling with the phone. "Hello?" Meena says.

"Hi. It's Peter," he says, pulling at the drawstring on his sweatshirt.

"Hi. What's up?" she asks.

"I just . . . thought I'd see what's going on with you tonight."

Meena's quiet at first. "Not much," she says.

He winces. "Well, you know Faith Saunders . . ." *Of course she does. She used to be friends with the girl!* "Well, she's having a party, and I was talking to Reed Frasier. He wants us to come."

Okay, so Reed didn't mention Meena. But Peter's sure Reed wouldn't mind if she came. Not that he actually expects her to say yes, anyway.

"I heard about that. Faith's parties are usually fun," Meena comments.

"So are you up for it?" he asks.

"No. I don't think so," Meena answers, on cue. "But you should go."

"Are you sure? Because if you want, I don't have to go, either," Peter says, hoping she knows he really means it. "We can hang out, do something else low-key."

"Peter, just go," she insists. "My brothers are here, and I want to hang out with them, anyway."

Peter wraps the sweatshirt's drawstring around his fingers. Can he trust that she'll really be okay? Well, he can't imagine anything would happen with Clayton if her brothers are there, at least.

"You're sure it's okay?" he asks again.

"I'm sure."

"Okay, but I'll call you first thing in the morning," Peter says. "I just . . . I just worry, you know."

"I know. Thanks."

• • •

Jane tugs nervously at her light blue V-necked sweater. She takes a barrette from her pocket and pulls back her hair. *No. Too conservative.* She unclips the barrette and lets her hair back down. *Don't freak out. It's just a party. Try to act like you know what you're doing.*

She knocks on the door. No answer. *Duh. People don't knock at these things. They just walk in.*

She turns the brass knob and cautiously opens the front door. It's not even nine, but the place is packed, and it reeks of beer. Bodies are crammed up against each other. The bass thump of the music vibrates in her chest. Some people dance; others shout conversations at one another. Jane searches the crowd for a familiar face. Actually, most are familiar. She's just not friends with any of them.

Hands in pockets. Hands out of pockets. Weight on right leg, then the left. *What was I thinking? I don't know how to do this. I don't belong here.*

"Hi, Jane," a voice shouts in her ear.

She turns around and sees Faith Saunders standing a few feet away. Aside from being a tall and athletic jock, Faith is gorgeous. Her long blond hair falls easily to her shoulders. She doesn't wear makeup, and even though she never dresses up, she still looks totally put together in jeans and a simple white T-shirt.

"Hi, Faith," Jane says, fumbling awkwardly with her hands. *She's probably wondering why I'm here. It's not like Faith invited me personally.*

"Glad you came," Faith says, shifting a shoulder to let someone pass. "I never see you around."

Hands back in pockets. "I don't go to many parties."

The door opens and three rowdy guys Jane recognizes from the swim team come in. Jane moves out of the way as Faith says hello. *How does she know all of these people?*

A nearby group of people jostle her and Jane gets shoved farther into the middle of the party.

"Where's the keg?" someone shouts.

I can't believe I'm actually at a keg party. She surveys the room for Reed or Peter but doesn't spot them.

As she makes her way through the crowd, she runs into Amy Santisi, whose eyes are glassy from drinking. "Hey, Jane," Amy says, clearly surprised to see her here. Jane has French with Amy and they've been partnered up on a few projects before but never talked much outside of class. "Jane, you've gotta see it—Shaheem Dobi and Bobby Scorella are doing keg stands. They're having a contest to see who can stay up the longest."

"They're doing what?" Jane asks.

"Keg stands. It's when . . . just come out back and watch," she says.

Suddenly Gemma Masters comes out of nowhere and nearly throws herself on Amy. "Oh my God. Can you believe Karyn went to Boston?" Gemma shrieks. "I think she's finally going to . . . you know."

"Yeah," Amy says. "Pretty big step."

Jane has no idea what they're talking about, but she doesn't care. On a normal Saturday night, she'd be quizzing her Academic Decathlon teammates about the natural resources in Africa. So whatever's happening right now has to be an improvement on that.

"Coming outside?" Amy asks.

"I'll be out in a sec," Jane says. "I just need to find a couple of people first."

Amy and Gemma keep heading toward the back, and Jane resumes searching the room for Peter and Reed. Someone knocks her from behind. "Sorry about—oh, hey, Jane. Sorry."

She looks up and sees a guy—Darren or Damien someone. *How did he know my name?* So many people. So many faces. Faces she's seen for years. But if they weren't on the Web site committee or in band or one of her other activities, they were just a blur. She walks over to an empty space in the corner. A sense of regret creeps through her. She's missed out on so much over the past few years, and what did it even get her? When she thinks of her future, she sees nothing. Empty space.

"Jane, over here!"

She turns in the direction of the voice and sees Peter Davis waving at her from the opposite wall. Reed and Jeremy Mandile are standing next to him.

Jane smiles in relief and weaves her way toward them through the crowd.

"You came!" Peter says.

"I came," she replies, shouting over the music.

"It's pretty cool, right?" Reed says, leaning close to her ear.

"Pretty cool for being here just ten minutes," she answers.

"You need a beer?" Jeremy asks.

"Of course she needs a beer," Peter says before she can answer.

Jane shrugs to Jeremy. "I guess I need a beer."

"Be right back," he says, easing himself through the mob.

"Beats working the night shift at TCBY," Reed jokes.

Jane scans the crowd. Wall-to-wall people. It's exactly how she'd pictured a high school party. Except for one thing. She never thought she'd be in the picture.

"Hey, Quinn," someone shouts.

Jane feels an immediate flush cover her body from head to toe. Her heart starts to pound. *He can't be here. No way. Oh my God . . . is that . . . ?*

Leaning against the back of a couch in the middle of the room is a tall, muscular figure. *Quinn was tall, but he was a beanpole. That can't be him.*

Jane squints. *No, that's definitely Quinn Saunders. I can't believe I'm under the same roof as Quinn Saunders.* He's wearing a blue crewneck sweater and faded jeans. That's weird—she's pretty sure she's never seen him dressed so casually. Quinn was always button-down shirts and pressed khakis all the way. But he sure has that same adorable, easy smile. God—it's been years, and that smile still turns her totally inside out.

As though sensing that he's being watched, Quinn turns his head. Their eyes meet.

Everything goes still for a second as Jane waits to see what he'll do. There's no way Quinn could remember her . . . is there?

And then it happens. The slight widening of his eyes, the twitch of his lips—an unmistakable expression of recognition. He waves at her, and as his smile broadens, the dimple appears that always used to make her melt.

A shock wave ripples through her body. She holds on to the back of Peter's wheelchair for balance. *Did he just wave at me?*

Yes, he did. And wait—that means she's supposed to respond.

Do something, her brain yells at her suddenly pointless limbs.

After what seems like ages, Jane manages to lift an arm to wave back. But the arm doesn't belong to her. It belongs to another Jane. One that's having the best night of her life.

• • •

Late Friday night, Karyn curls herself comfortably inside T. J.'s arms. His roommate has gone home for Thanksgiving, so they've got the room to themselves. It's quiet and dark. He pulls her to his chest so his chin rests on top of her head. She's always liked the way he holds her. Like nothing else could fit.

T. J. snuggles closer. "Mmm."

Karyn smiles to herself. Ever since she arrived, he's been telling her how glad he is that she decided to come. How he couldn't imagine a more perfect girl in his life. It's made her even more excited to tell him what she's decided.

At first, she'd planned on telling him as soon as she got here. She just wanted to do it right away. But then he'd told her that he had reservations for a nice Italian restaurant, and she figured it made sense to wait. That way it could be like she imagined—first a romantic dinner, and then . . . well, what she'd come here to do.

Unfortunately, the restaurant T. J. picked didn't turn out to be all that romantic—just dark. And kind of crowded and smoky. But it's not like T. J. knows that she wants to . . . that tonight is finally . . . the night.

Karyn shuts her eyes and takes a deep breath. She wants to get up and brush the garlic smell from her breath, but that would ruin the moment. And the moment is important. It's crucial.

This is exactly the way I wanted it to be. Losing my virginity to someone who loves me. Someone I trust. I know I'm ready for this. Just tell him.

"T. J.," she whispers.

"Mmm?"

"I've been thinking."

"'Bout what, babe?"

Karyn pulls his arm tighter around her waist. "About you and me."

"I think about us all the time," he says.

It's time. Don't be scared. You can trust T. J. "I've been thinking about sex."

She feels T. J. shift. He raises himself on one arm. Karyn rolls over onto her back so their eyes meet.

He looks at her softly. Intently. "Yeah?" he says.

She lifts her head so her lips practically touch his. "I'm ready." That's it. She can't take it back. She rests her head on the pillow again.

T. J. squeezes her tight. "Are you sure?" he asks. So sweet, so tender.

"Yes, I'm sure," she says, even though suddenly there's a giant lump in her throat. Nervous. She's just nervous. Everyone is, for the first time. "It just seems, you know, silly to wait any longer." Something heavy and uncomfortable secures itself in her stomach. Karyn stiffens. *Relax, Karyn. This is what you want.*

T. J.'s eyes gleam with excitement, then he frowns. "If I had known, I could have made everything special," he says. "I could have gotten a hotel room or something."

"This is special," she says, feeling the lump get bigger. "Your dorm is practically empty. And I like the idea of being in your bed."

"I could have at least bought a bottle of champagne. Some flowers."

Karyn shakes her head. "This is fine. You're all I need." She presses her body against his. Now that she's said it, she just wants to do it. Everything will be perfect then. The way it's supposed to be.

Karyn moves her lips up to his, and they kiss for a long time.

She fights back the lump, the fear that's behind it. Once she's done this, all the doubts will disappear.

CHAPTER ELEVEN

"Earth to Jane."

"Wh-what?" Jane stammers.

"Hello—you there?"

Jane pulls her attention from Quinn Saunders and looks down at Peter, who's wearing an amused grin. She glances quickly at Reed and Jeremy and sees they have matching smiles. Jane's cheeks grow even warmer.

"What's that guy got that we don't?" Jeremy asks, handing her a beer.

"What do you—what guy?" Jane says, her palms getting clammy.

"The guy who put you in a temporary trance," Jeremy says.

"Let's hope it's temporary," Peter adds with a laugh.

Jane licks her lips. Was it really that obvious? *Oh my God. I must have looked so pathetic, just staring at him. I hope I at least kept my tongue in my mouth.*

"Quinn Saunders looks a lot different than he did three years ago," Reed says, elbowing Jane. "Not so much the study geek."

Jane nods, still in shock. It's true. Even his posture seems different. He always used to stand perfectly tall, rigid and alert. Now he's slouching against the couch.

And he waved at me. He actually waved hello.

Jane forces herself not to look back in his direction. She lifts the yellow plastic cup full of beer and takes a sip. The fizz tickles her nose. She takes another sip. It's not so bad, actually.

She's about to tell Jeremy that when she feels a tap on her shoulder. "Jane?"

Jane sucks in her breath. It's Quinn—she knows that voice as well as she did three years ago. She turns around and there he is. He actually walked across the room to talk to her.

And just like that, all of her carefully honed language skills fly out the window.

Say hi. You can do it. One stupid word.

"Hi," she blurts out.

"Hey," he says. "Wow, it's been a while. How's everything going?"

She can barely hear him, between the noise level in the room and the sound of her own heart in her ears. At least it gives her an excuse to stall. "What?" she says.

He smiles. There's that dimple again. "I said," he begins, leaning closer to her, "how's everything going?"

Oh God—his face is inches away from hers. She can't do this. She can't possibly think of what to say to—

173

Something sharp strikes her ankle. Jane winces, then glances at Peter. Did he actually just roll into her with his wheelchair on purpose?

Jane looks back at Quinn, takes a deep breath. "Oh . . . uh, things are good. Really good. How's Stanford?" *Why did you ask that? You know he doesn't go to Stanford anymore.*

"Actually, I transferred to UCLA. I love it there."

Jane's mouth drops open. *UCLA? A state university? I don't get it—why would he leave Stanford for a state school?*

"Any idea where you're headed next year?"

Jane struggles to compose herself. It was hard enough acting sane around Quinn in the first place, but now that he's just thrown her that curveball, she's *really* lost her powers of speech.

"Um, I'm actually not sure yet," she mumbles. Something really weird must have happened for him to end up at UCLA, but still—there's no way she can tell Quinn that she's actually headed a big fat nowhere next fall.

"Where?" he shouts.

"Not sure," she says a little louder.

"That's probably better," Quinn says, keeping his voice raised so she can hear him. "That was my big mistake. I wanted to go to Stanford since freshman year of high school. Everyone else wanted me to go there, too—my parents were so hyped up on it. By the time I was applying, I didn't even remember what I liked about the school, but I just went through with it, anyway."

Jane takes another sip of beer. Works up the courage for her next question. "So why did you leave?" she asks.

Quinn rolls his eyes. "The second I got to that place, I knew I'd made a big mistake. But I stuck it out, took a bunch of premed classes, joined some clubs. One month into my first semester, I knew I had to leave."

Quinn Saunders made a mistake. Why am I having such a hard time believing that?

"Didn't your parents flip?" she asks.

"Yeah." He shrugs. "But they had to deal with it."

Jane nods, even though she doesn't really understand. *My parents would never deal. They'd have me locked up before they'd let me go to a state university.*

"Hey, is Bonnebaker still doing the Web site?" he asks.

Jane smiles. "Yeah."

"And Motti? She's still doing Academic Decathlon?"

Jane gives another nod.

"Oh, man, you've gotta fill me in on this stuff," he says with a laugh. "Do you want to go where the music isn't blaring in our ears?"

Jane's throat suddenly feels dry. She takes a long gulp of her beer, then glances at Peter, Reed, and Jeremy. They're talking to each other, something about where to get pizza late at night. Peter gives her a quick wink.

"Sure, okay," she says, turning back to Quinn.

"Come on," he says, taking her by the elbow. They walk down a long hall that extends off the living room. There's a couple leaning against the wall engaged in a kissing marathon.

"I forgot what high school parties are like," Quinn tells her. He pauses and looks at her intently. "But I'm glad I'm here. It's really cool to see you."

Jane wonders if there's a part of her that *isn't* blushing right now.

Quinn opens a door and guides her into what looks like a den. A group of people sit in a circle, playing some kind of game. Probably a drinking game, since they've got a million cups of beer. Quinn leads Jane past them to a soft suede couch facing a window. Outside, the moon sits up in the sky, perfectly round. Jane pinches her elbow. *Is this real? Is Quinn Saunders really sitting two inches from me? Just talk to him. He's a person, Jane, not a god.*

"So how long are you home for?" she asks.

"A little while, actually. I'm going to Australia for a zoology project next semester, and I'm sticking around Winetka Falls until then, taking some time to chill."

"Zoology?" Jane blurts out, unable to hide her surprise.

Quinn laughs, then runs a hand through his blond hair. "Yeah, I know, not what people who knew me back then would expect." He stares out the window, his expression growing serious. "But I guess there's a lot about me now that no one expected."

"When did—I mean, how did everything change for you?" she asks.

He presses his lips together. "For a while, it wasn't so easy getting everyone to see that I was sick of just doing what they expected," he says. "My parents, teachers, friends—they all had it set for me. Where I'd go to school, what I'd do when I got there . . . I don't know, it probably sounds lame to you, but I kind of lost it."

Jane can't believe what he's saying. It's like he took the words right out of her own head. "It—it doesn't sound lame at all," she says softly.

Quinn turns his eyes from the window, focusing his gaze back on Jane. "Thanks," he says. "That means a lot, coming from you."

"From . . . me?"

"Yeah, totally. God, you always had it all together, even freshman year." He shakes his head. "Not me. I pretty much stopped functioning at Stanford." He leans toward her, lowering his voice. "Do you know that I actually *failed* a test? I mean, I'd never even gotten lower than a B-plus in high school. For a while, I just reeled. I thought everything was over. But then I started to see that, you know, yeah— I'd failed a test. But the world was still going on around me. All life didn't cease to exist just because Quinn Saunders failed a test."

Jane blinks. The way he says it . . . it does sound pretty crazy, putting so much importance on a test grade. But the test *she* messed up wasn't just for one class in school. Failing at the SATs is a whole different level. Isn't it?

The people playing the drinking game burst out laughing. Jane and Quinn look over and see one guy chugging from a pitcher.

"So . . . what happened next?" Jane asks.

Quinn tilts his head. "First, there was a lot of fighting. With teachers, and mostly with my parents. But finally they saw how miserable I was. They got that Stanford was their dream, not mine. And they let me transfer to UCLA. It's not like I don't still care about my grades, but I have more of a balance now. No more of that crazed feeling of just running from one place to the next without even stopping to breathe."

"Like you're a robot," Jane says, nodding. "Like you're this robot that belongs to everyone else, and you're just doing whatever they programmed you to do."

Quinn lets out a sigh. "Exactly," he says. He frowns at her. "So is that how you feel?" he asks. "I mean, you always seemed to have everything under control. It looked like—I don't know, like it was easy for you."

Jane chokes out a laugh. "That's what I always thought about you," she says.

"Really?"

"Yeah, really."

They're silent for a moment, and Jane just stares at the moon, trying to process everything.

"If it means anything, I've turned out okay," Quinn says finally. "I'm having a great time with this zoology program, and I'm really psyched for the trip to Australia. Like

I said, the sky didn't fall because I decided to slow things down a little." He moves closer to her, rests a hand gently on her shoulder. "You're a great person, Jane, and if you feel the way I used to—well, I just don't want you to go through what I did at Stanford. Follow your heart, okay?"

Jane swallows hard. No one has ever made her feel like she's not the only one trapped in the commotion of her brain. Quinn has been there. And he got out. Now he's doing exactly what he wants with his life.

If he did it . . . then why can't she?

Quinn is close. So close, she can hear his breathing. So close, she can imagine what it would be like to touch him. The warmth of his hand through her sweater radiates heat down her whole arm.

"Jane, I . . . ," Quinn begins. He stops, his blue eyes looking at her nervously.

Go after what you want, a voice in Jane's head instructs her. Maybe it's the beer, since she never drinks, or maybe it's how intoxicating Quinn's description of finding freedom was. Jane doesn't know what gives her the nerve, but before she's had a chance to think of an answer, she's leaning across the sofa . . . and kissing Quinn Saunders.

Their lips meet. His arms encircle her, pulling her closer. Jane allows herself one last thought before banishing her brain from the moment—*Mmm.*

• • •

Late Friday night, Peter sits in his wheelchair, staring

179

out his bedroom window. Even though it's nearly three in the morning, he doesn't feel like getting in bed. His mind is working overtime, recalling fragments of the evening. Partying used to mean getting too wasted to have a coherent conversation. Peter ingested his share of beer tonight, but at least he wasn't drinking one after another and then going around spray painting mailboxes. He had hung out with Reed and Jeremy for most of the party, and then Danny had actually shown up, with Cori Lerner. They'd all talked for a while, and Peter and Danny talked about maybe meeting up at the mall tomorrow.

He places his palms on the tops of his thighs. Rubs them back and forth. The soft corduroy heats up his hands, creating static. One day the heat is going to penetrate his skin. *I know I'm gonna feel again. I just know it.*

Peter gazes out the window at his backyard, at the tree he used to climb as a kid. Things were so different back then. All he did was play ball, climb trees. Then a little later, that turned into skipping school and getting into fistfights. It all changed after his tenth birthday. After that day in the basement. Before then, he had lots of friends. Barely fought with any of them. Didn't need to. Then he stopped hanging out with those friends. They drifted apart.

Peter looks at his hands. They're shaking. *Seven years since we were all together. Seven years since that day. Do they think about it, too?*

He pictures the look on Karyn's face at his window the

180

other night. Her mouth hung open slightly and her eyes just stared. Peter knew not to ask questions. Karyn didn't want to reveal anything. She just wanted to be there. With him.

That's exactly how Peter felt tonight, hanging out with Reed and Jeremy, and Danny. It felt normal. Which is so weird, since he hasn't exchanged more than a few words with them in years. It's only been recently, since they've bumped into each other, that they've had actual conversations. But in a bizarre way it feels natural to be with them. Like they're supposed to be together.

If anything, we should be kept as far away from each other as possible. Last time we were together . . .

Peter shakes the thought from his head. He stretches his arms. *Maybe I'll just rest here. Just as comfortable . . .*

The telephone rings, and he jerks himself awake. He looks at his clock. Three-fifteen. *Who's calling this late?*

He reaches for the receiver. "Hello?"

"Peter, it's me," a barely audible voice says.

"Meena? Is everything okay?"

"I heard a noise." She chokes on a sob. "A footstep outside my door."

Peter's heart stops. "Are you alone? Let me get my dad. He'll have a squad car over there in five minutes."

"No, wait!" Meena blurts out, in a loud whisper. "I think it's my brother. Let me check."

Peter hears the muffled sounds of a hand over the receiver.

"It's my brother Jonah," Meena says, coming back on

181

the line. "He was walking to the bathroom. I woke up and I was so out of it that I forgot he was here."

Peter lets out his breath.

"I guess I just panicked," she says, her voice still shaky.

"If I could drive, I'd be right over, Meena," Peter says, wiping a layer of sweat from his upper lip.

"That's okay. When I called, I thought . . . I don't know. It was a stupid mistake. I'm fine."

She doesn't sound fine. She sounds like someone's dangling her over the edge of a cliff.

"I can come over first thing in the morning," he says, feeling a familiar frustration with his stupid, useless legs.

"No, I'm sorry for calling you so late. It was stupid."

"No, it wasn't stupid, Meena. You can call me anytime. But will you do me a favor?"

"Peter, I know what you're going to say. Please don't."

Peter stares at a branch sagging from a birch tree in his backyard. It nearly broke off in a storm last month. One more storm and the thing will definitely come down.

"Meena, you need to talk to someone."

"I'm talking to you," she replies.

Peter leans his forehead against his palm. He knows how badly she doesn't want him to tell anyone about this, but if he can't convince her to do it on her own soon—he's going to have to do something. This is obviously way more serious than either of them can handle on their own.

• • •

There is something Reed has to take care of. But he's not sure exactly what. If he could just get out of this basement, he's sure he'd know what he's supposed to be doing.

He turns around, looking for a door, but all he sees are cement walls. It feels like he's been down here for hours. Down in the cold. In the darkness. The only light comes from a rectangular window near the ceiling.

Exhausted, he sits on the floor and leans against a wooden support beam. The grainy floor rubs through his jeans.

Someone starts to laugh. Reed whips his head in the direction of the sound and sees Karyn. She's sitting next to him, tossing a football between her hands. Her dirty-blond hair falls carelessly over her face. How did she get here?

T. J., catch, she says, *throwing the football to Reed.*

He catches it.

I'm Reed.

Throw it back, she says, *holding out her hands.*

He tosses the ball and she catches it. Karyn laughs harder, and the room fills with light. Slowly at first, until the darkness is replaced with a warm glow, like a summer afternoon. Now she'll see Reed. She'll recognize her mistake.

The light around them keeps getting brighter. Reed leans close so his lips are inches from hers. Karyn. He's always been in love with her. But something has held him back. Until now.

Reed takes the football from Karyn's hands and tosses it across the room. It rolls across the floor and stops at the base of a closet, one Reed hadn't seen before. He stares at the closet doors. What's inside?

Karyn taps him on the shoulder. He looks at her. Forget about the closet. He's with Karyn. They're alone. Together.

He lunges toward her, covering her body with his own. Her giggles subside when he places his mouth on hers. The kiss starts off soft. Then the softness evolves into longer, more eager kisses. Reed can't imagine any other feeling. He's with the girl he loves. Finally.

T. J., not here. *Karyn giggles.*

She still thinks that Reed is T. J. He knows he should pull away, but he can't. Her lips are so sweet. So gentle.

I've been waiting to kiss her my whole life. I'm not going to let T. J. screw this up. He gets in the way of everything.

What the hell is going on here?

Reed and Karyn look in the direction of the voice. It's Reed's father. He stands over them, his scowl deep and frightening.

I—I was just, *Reed stutters,* I mean, we were just . . .

T. J., this behavior is unacceptable.

What? Reed's father thinks that Reed is T. J., too?

You don't bring girls to a dark basement, T. J.

Dad, I'm R—

I don't want any excuses.

Reed trembles. His father stands only a foot away. How can he not tell his sons apart?

Rules are rules, T. J., *his father shouts.* What's so hard about following them?

I'm not T. J., *he screams.* I'm Reed.

Don't blame this on your brother. Don't you dare. He's better than you. Smarter. He'd never do something like this.

A small clicking noise comes from behind him and Reed turns around. Karyn is standing in front of the closet. It's open. Tears run down her face. Her hair, the same hair that tickled his face, is knotted together in clumps. She's holding something. It's black and shiny.

A gun. Her hand trembles. She lifts the gun and aims it over Reed's shoulder.

Karyn, no, *Reed shouts.*

She nods in Reed's direction. Your father can't treat you this way, T. J.

No!

Too late. Click.

Reed bolts upright in bed, his body covered in sweat. He rubs his temples. *Hot. It's too hot in here.* He gets out of bed and opens his window. Leans his head as far outside as possible. The cold night air slices into his skin.

A nightmare. It was just a nightmare. But it's more than that. Deep in his gut, he knows he's headed for serious trouble.

• • •

Saturday morning, Karyn shifts her shoulders from side to side. Her body feels tight and uncomfortable. Unfamiliar. She opens her eyes and sees T. J.'s jeans slung over a chair. On the floor is her sweater. Her belt.

185

She presses her eyes shut, hoping that when she opens them again, she'll be somewhere else. Not in Boston. Not at BC. Not in T. J.'s bed.

T. J. breathes heavily. The stench of his breath stings her nose. Makes her want to gag. She shifts her shoulders again, trying to free herself from his hold. Impossible. His heavy arm is slung over her waist.

Why does she feel this way? Like her body has been turned inside out. Nothing is right. Not like she thought it would be. *Sex was supposed to make everything fall into place.*

But instead it just ripped everything apart even more. Ripped *her* apart.

Karyn blinks back tears and manages to slide out from under T. J.'s arm and place her bare feet on the floor. The cold shoots up her legs, biting her ankles, her knees.

"Morning, babe."

Karyn stiffens. Her back is to T. J.

Turn around. You have to look at him.

But her body is a dead weight. If she turns around, she'll have to see his face. Then she'll remember last night. His expression while they were . . . he was so happy. He kept murmuring her name, saying he loved her. And all she could do was bite down on her lip to keep from screaming at him to stop, to get away from her. It hurt—it hurt in so many ways, like she'd never be whole again.

His hand grabs hold of her forearm and he pulls her down on the bed. "You're up early," he says, nuzzling her back.

Karyn shrinks from his touch. "Yeah, I was just gonna go to the bathroom."

"Don't go," he says, reaching an arm around her waist.

On the nightstand is the candle he'd lit last night. The sweet smell of the wax reaches her nostrils. She's going to puke.

"I have to go," she says loudly, and stands up.

T. J. pulls her back down. The mattress molds to the contours of her body. It draws her deeper into the bed. Karyn keeps her eyes fixed on the ceiling. *What did I do? Sex was going to make everything okay. Make me realize that I'm in love with T. J., the right person, the one who wants me. Make me realize that kissing Reed was a stupid mistake.*

But the scariest part of last night was the one thought that had penetrated through all of the pain and fear. The one truly clear realization: *This should have been Reed.*

T. J. presses his face close. Karyn doesn't move. His coarse skin stings her face. He rolls his body on top of her, touching . . . moving. Too close. He doesn't belong there. *The second it began, I wanted it to end. Needed it to end.*

"No," she moans, about to cry. "No, please, stop."

T. J. pulls back, a look of confusion spreading across his face. Karyn looks up at him. The person she lost her virginity to. Someone who tells her he loves her but doesn't know the first thing about her. Doesn't understand what makes her sad. Doesn't know the right things to say when she's upset.

A sob escapes her throat. *He was supposed to be the*

187

one. Now my body . . . I feel . . . I just can't be near him.

Why did she take this stupid trip? Everything about Boston—everything about T. J.—repulses her. How did she talk herself back into believing she's in love with him, after that kiss with Reed? She doesn't love T. J. She loves Reed—and she's just done the one thing to ensure she'll never be able to be with him.

"What's wrong?" T. J. asks, reaching for her arm. "Are you okay?"

Karyn shakes her head. She can't speak. All the thought she'd put into losing her virginity. All the time she'd spent convincing herself sex with T. J. was right.

"Are you sick?" he asks with a concerned frown.

"No," she says.

"Babe, what's the matter? Let's talk about it," he pleads.

Karyn just shakes her head. *No going back. It's over.* "I think we should . . ."

"We should what?"

No. No. Sex was supposed to make things right. I wasn't going to be like my mom—I was going to give myself to someone who wanted me, someone who would never leave me. But why did I never stop and think about how wrong it is to do this with someone I don't really want, no matter how devoted he is to me?

"We should what?" T. J. prods.

The room turns unbearably cold. "I think we should break up."